Twelve military heroes.
Twelve indomitable heroines.
*One **UNIFORMLY HOT!** miniseries.*

Don't miss Harlequin Blaze's first 12-book
continuity series, featuring irresistible soldiers
from all branches of the armed forces.

Watch for:

***LETTERS FROM HOME** by Rhonda Nelson*
(Army Rangers—June 2009)

***THE SOLDIER** by Rhonda Nelson*
(Special Forces—July 2009)

***STORM WATCH** by Jill Shalvis*
(National Guard—August 2009)

***HER LAST LINE OF DEFENSE** by Marie Donovan*
(Green Berets—September 2009)

***RIPPED!** by Jennifer LaBrecque*
(Paratrooper—October 2009)

***SEALED AND DELIVERED** by Jill Monroe*
(Navy SEALs—November 2009)

***CHRISTMAS MALE** by Cara Summers*
(Military Police—December 2009)

Uniformly Hot!
The Few. The Proud. The Sexy as Hell.

Dear Reader,

When I learned the Harlequin Blaze editors were putting together a yearlong military-themed miniseries, I immediately threw my writing hat into the ring. I come from a long line of army men—my husband is an army veteran, and several of his family served, as well. And I really wanted to write about a Green Beret hero. My mother was a social worker in Vietnam during the war and knew several Green Beret soldiers. She used to tell me stories about them, and as I have learned, not much was an exaggeration. Green Berets then and Green Berets now are smart, tough, multilingual, highly trained U.S. Army Special Forces soldiers whose motto is De Oppresso Liber—to free the oppressed.

My weary Green Beret hero, Luc Boudreau, has been through several difficult deployments and all he wants to do is go home to his family. But heroine Claire Cook needs survival training, and Luc is the only one who can teach her. Duty keeps him from home once more, but maybe he can make a new home with Claire. After all, life is more than just survival!

Happy reading!

Marie Donovan

Marie Donovan

HER LAST LINE OF DEFENSE

HARLEQUIN®

TORONTO • NEW YORK • LONDON
AMSTERDAM • PARIS • SYDNEY • HAMBURG
STOCKHOLM • ATHENS • TOKYO • MILAN • MADRID
PRAGUE • WARSAW • BUDAPEST • AUCKLAND

Recycling programs
for this product may
not exist in your area.

ISBN-13: 978-0-373-79497-3

HER LAST LINE OF DEFENSE

Copyright © 2009 by Marie Donovan.

www.eHarlequin.com

Printed in U.S.A.

ABOUT THE AUTHOR

Marie Donovan is a Chicago-area native, who got her fill of tragedies and unhappy endings by majoring in opera/vocal performance and Spanish literature. As an antidote to all that gloom, she read romance novels voraciously throughout college and graduate school.

Donovan worked for a large suburban public library for ten years as both a cataloguer and a bilingual Spanish storytime presenter. She graduated magna cum laude with two bachelor's degrees from a Midwestern liberal arts university and speaks six languages. She enjoys reading, gardening and yoga.

Please visit the author's Web site at www.mariedonovan.com and also her Sizzling Pens group blog at www.sizzlingpens.blogspot.com.

Books by Marie Donovan

HARLEQUIN BLAZE
204—HER BODY OF WORK
302—HER BOOK OF PLEASURE
371—BARE NECESSITIES
470—MY SEXY GREEK SUMMER

In memory of two humble men: my grandpa Oz,
who merely "cleaned up in Europe";
and Great-Uncle Richard,
who "watched the fireworks" while trapped
under a bush on a hill in the Philippines.

And to my husband, who tells me you can
indeed sleep on the back of an armored tank
if you get tired enough.

God bless all our soldiers.

1

"No, no! Hell, no! Not just hell no, fu—"

"At ease, Sergeant!" It wasn't a suggestion.

Luc Boudreaux clamped his mouth shut and wondered who in the hell he had pissed off badly enough to lead him to this. He thought he'd made it through his Afghan tour of duty without stepping on his crank. He'd stayed away from the local girls, avoided shooting anyone who didn't deserve it and brought some decent health care to several tribes whose only technology was Soviet-era weaponry.

He took a deep breath. "Sir, may I ask why I am being selected for this task?"

Captain Olson, his commanding officer snorted. "Can the 'sir' shit—you haven't called me 'sir' in years. Now pull the stick out of your ass and sit down."

Luc dropped into the beat-up office chair and stared at his boss across the equally beat-up desk. Special Forces spent their budget on gear, not furniture. "Okay, Olie, what the hell?" He spread his hands wide in frustration.

Magnus Olson, or "Olie" as he was known to his

men and half of Afghanistan, stroked the long blond beard that made him look like a recruiting poster for Viking pillagers. Luc guessed his own black beard made him a pirate poster boy. "Like I was trying to say before you ripped me a new one, here's the rest of the deal, and I have to admit it's a crappy one—you train Congressman Cook's daughter in jungle survival skills, and the fine congressman won't torpedo your career."

"What?" Luc leaped to his feet.

Olie let him blow off several choice remarks before lifting a meaty hand. "Okay, okay. Sit down, Rage, and I'll go over this again real slow with you."

For once, Luc was living up to his nickname of the Ragin' Cajun. Most of the time it was a team joke since he was usually a mellow guy. But now, no. The battle lines were drawn.

Olie reached behind him, pulled a beer out of the minifridge and tossed the bottle to Luc. "Drink up. We deserve it."

Luc popped the cap and took a long pull of the icy brew, suddenly weary. "Seriously, why me? Get a jungle survival school instructor. I have lots and lots of leave coming my way, and I need to get back to Louisiana." His parents and grandparents had had serious home damage from the last hurricane that blew through, and Luc was going to help them rebuild.

"'It has to be you, it has to be you-u-u-u,'" Olie crooned to the old show-tune melody. "You're the only guy I know who survived the jungles of San Lucas de la Selva alone for more than a month with only the clothes on his back and a machete."

"Oh, *mon Dieu.*" Luc sat up in horror. "His daughter is going to San Lucas de la Selva?"

Olie nodded, all traces of laughter gone from his face. "That she is. The lovely country San Lucas de la Selva, joke of the jungle, armpit of the Amazon."

Hellish nightmare here on earth was more like it. Luc was firmly convinced that his survival—and a close thing that had been—had rested entirely on his grandmother's daily rosary for his health and the fact that he shared a name with *le bon père* Saint Lucas of the Jungle, the rugged nineteenth century priest who had disappeared into the jungle to bring the natives to Christ. Three years later, explorers from the outpost had been stunned to find Saint Lucas alive and well, ministering to his local parishioners. Every stinking, nasty day in that jungle, Luc had prayed to Saint Lucas to, well, basically intercede for his sorry ass and get him the hell out of there. He'd prayed for other things, too, but they hadn't been granted.

And now it looked as if Saint Lucas was collecting on the promises Luc had made him. "This girl, she can't know what it's like down there, or else she wouldn't even think of going." Luc still got a chill down his spine when he saw a map of the Amazon.

"According to the congressman, his late wife grew up in a missionary settlement in San Lucas, where her parents were doctors."

"They lived there on purpose?" Luc couldn't even imagine. "And why can't the congressman talk his daughter out of it? Is she dumb or something? Has a death wish?"

"He's tried everything short of having the State Department pull her passport but she has apparently grown up on exotic tales of the jungle." Olie waggled his fingers in a fake-mystic way. "She's signed up to teach the locals in the same settlement—wants to follow in the family footsteps."

"And she's picking the jungle over politics."

Olie laughed. "Might be fewer snakes in the jungle."

Luc snorted. "So what the hell do I do, Olie? This jerk-off would really screw me over?"

"In a heartbeat." His CO looked away and drank some beer, flicking his forefinger against his thumb.

"What is it?" Olie only did that little thing with his hand when he was jittery.

"Nothing."

"Olie…" Luc cajoled him.

"Nothing. I said it was nothing, and I mean nothing, Boudreaux."

"No way." Luc shook his head in amazement. "He threatened you and the rest of the team, too, didn't he? And you didn't want to tell me 'cuz that would pressure me to agree."

"In case you haven't noticed, Sergeant Boudreaux, I am a big boy whose career doesn't depend on the good opinion of some shit-eating congressman—and yours doesn't, either."

"Shit," Luc said. He never figured on making general someday but didn't want to leave the army before he was good and ready. Or slink out with his tail between his legs as if he'd been dishonorably discharged. And to let Olie and the team get screwed over, too?

"I'll do it."

"You sure?" Olie gave him a steely glare.

"I'm sure." Luc managed to fake a laugh. "Maybe once Daddy's Little Princess sees what survival training is like, she'll go back to the snakes in Washington, D.C."

"YOU MADE ARRANGEMENTS for what?" Claire Cook dug her nails into her palms and winced at the pain.

"Jungle survival lessons." Her father gave her a wide smile and helped himself to a glass of sweet tea from the pitcher in the cherry-paneled, extra-large refrigerator. "Ah, delicious. Did you brew mint leaves into it, as well? Very refreshing."

Claire had been a politician's daughter long enough to know tap dancing when she saw it. "Survival lessons?" she prompted.

Her dad set down the glass and dropped his soothing tone. "Since you have decided this is your course of action, foolish as it may be, I am helping you to implement your choice in the safest way possible."

"Dad, really. The settlement at Río San Lucas is its

own little town—just like Cooksville." Their hometown was named after their ancestor, who helped settle central Virginia before the Revolutionary War. The redbrick house they were standing in had been commandeered by the British as a barracks during that war and barely escaped being burned by the Yankees during what her grandfather Cook had always referred to as the War of Northern Aggression.

But her dad was on a roll. "Cooksville isn't surrounded by deadly rain forest, killer snakes and venomous spiders."

Claire made a face. There he was harping on the snakes and spiders again, just because she didn't even like the supposedly harmless daddy longlegs spiders. Maybe she should try killing them on her own rather than yelling for their housekeeper, Louella. She flinched at a tickle on her neck and realized it was a stray dark hair falling out of her ponytail. She really had to get over that.

"Not to mention jaguars, feral pigs and half-naked tribesmen who would be more than happy to add an exotically beautiful young girl to their harem, or squad of wives, or concubine crew, or whatever they call it down there."

Claire had to roll her eyes. Brown hair, brown eyes and brown freckles scattered across a nose that hovered on the edge of snub was hardly exotic. And honestly, she'd had plenty of practice fighting off overly amorous men among the suit-wearing tribes of the

Potomac River. A couple she hadn't fought at all, but her dad didn't need to know that.

"I will be fine," she enunciated carefully. "So thank you, but no thanks. Dr. Schmidt will show me the ropes once I get down there and I won't have any problems."

"Claire, Claire, Claire." Her father shook his carefully coiffed silver head in what she figured was mock ruefulness.

"Dad, Dad, Dad." She copied him right back.

He dropped the Mr. Nice Dad act and pulled on his congressman face—not the kindly, wise face the cameras saw, but the face his opponents saw when they tried to block his bills or basically thwart his not-inconsiderable will. "You will take this training, or you won't go to San Lucas. Not to teach, not to visit, not even to fly over it."

"And I told *you,* if you try to pull my passport, I will go to the media. I'm sure that TV reporter you accidentally called a 'slime-sucking son of a bitch' on live feed would be happy to interview me."

Her old man pulled his face into a half grin. "Ah, you wound me, Claire. To think that I of all people would be so obvious, and after all these years in politics, no less."

A knot tightened in her stomach. "If you're not going to be obvious, then what?"

"Dr. Schmidt is coming to the States on a fundraising lecture tour in January, isn't he?"

"Yes." Claire eyed him narrowly.

"And the settlement gets most of its funding from American donations, doesn't it?"

"Yes," she muttered. Dammit, she knew what was coming.

"If the kind European Dr. Schmidt is found to have some problem that might prevent his American visa from being approved, perhaps the nasty rumor of association with the narcoterrorists in the south of San Lucas—"

"Dad!" Claire's chest tightened. "Dr. Schmidt has never associated with the drug runners—never!"

"Come on, Claire, we both know he doesn't ask many questions when some scumbag shows up with a mysterious gunshot wound he got while 'cleaning his automatic rifle.'" Her dad made air quotes with his fingers. "Your grandfather did the same thing when he ran the settlement, so don't try to tell me different."

Claire pursed her lips. "The settlement is neutral territory down there. That's why they need me as a teacher. The local villagers know it's safe to send their children for schooling so they can get an education, have a better life than what their parents had."

"And do what? Move to the city where they can live in slums and pick over the garbage dump for food?" Dad shook his head. "Your mother and I had this discussion a million times. What if they are better off in the jungle, doing what their ancestors have done for thousands of years?"

"And what did Mom say? She was the one who grew up in the settlement."

"Your mother was adopted into the tribe, knew the languages and cultures and was generally regarded as a world expert on San Lucas de la Selva, but even *she* didn't know the answers. How do you expect to?"

This was what was so infuriating about arguing with her father. He had the politician's trick of turning her argument back on her and twisting her words all around. She resorted to what *did* work: stubbornness. "I don't expect to fix everything. I expect to go."

"My God, you're pigheaded." He shook his head. "Just like your mother and grandfather. All right. You'll go—if you pass the survival training."

Claire protested but he held up his hand, his blue eyes blazing. "You are my only child, the only child of your mother, and I will be damned if I put you on a plane to the dangerous jungle when you can't even make yourself kill a harmless spider here in Virginia. I'm willing to let you go, but not as some lamb to the jungle slaughter."

"Fine." Claire gritted her teeth and relaxed. She'd been a Girl Scout, knew how to build a fire, find out which way was north. This would be similar, only designed for a more tropical climate than central Virginia. "How hard can it be?"

Her dad smiled, but it was his sharky smile that Claire had never seen directed at her before. "How hard can it be?" he mocked. "I guess you'll have to ask

Sergeant First Class Luc Boudreaux. He's the Green Beret soldier who will be training you."

"OH, WOW. YOUR dad said 'Green Beret Sergeant First Class Boudreaux'?" Claire's best friend Janey Merrick stopped midjog and bit her lip.

"Yes, why?" Claire sucked in some oxygen, glad for the break. Janey was in much better shape than she was, being an army first lieutenant at the Pentagon attached to some general's staff. She had gone through the Reserve Officers Training Corps at the University of Virginia, where she and Claire had met.

Janey pushed her light brown bangs off her forehead while Claire drank some water. "Green Berets are trained for anything and everything, but their specialty is working with and training indigenous forces. Back in the Vietnam War, they were the jungle warfare specialists—they called them the snake eaters."

"Snake eaters?" Claire's stomach pitched.

"They've branched out since, especially to desert and mountain warfare, but they are some of the toughest SOBs in the army." Janey eyed her. "Well, if you have a Green Beret sergeant first-class training you, I won't worry so much. Those guys know everything. You'll learn how to take care of yourself or die trying."

"Oh, Janey." Claire staggered to a park bench and collapsed. "Why did my dad do this to me? Am I going to have to eat snakes?"

Her friend laughed. "Because he doesn't want you

to go, and yes, probably. But they taste kind of like tough chicken—so I've been told. Hey, and here I was complaining about a desk job."

Claire sat up straight. When had she become a whiner? Whiners never won. "I'm still going to do it. I can eat snakes. I can survive in the jungle. I can do it." She jumped to her feet and jogged in place, ignoring the burn in her thigh muscles. "Let's go!"

Janey shook her head and smiled. "By the time you come back, you'll be able to kick my ass. Come on, soldier girl. I'll teach you some running cadences— they'll help you breathe better. Repeat after me— okay?" She broke into a jog and Claire followed. "I wanna be an Airborne Ranger."

"I wanna be an Airborne Ranger," Claire managed to gasp.

"Live the life of sex and danger."

"Live the life of—what?" Claire stopped again.

"Sex and danger, Claire, sex and danger. They go hand-in-hand for soldiers. The danger gets their adrenaline all revved up and they burn it off with sex." Janey grinned. "Remember that time we were supposed to go shopping and I told you I had to work all weekend? Well, last year I'd gone out a couple times with this one marine right before he shipped out."

"Yes?" Claire lifted an eyebrow.

Janey wiggled her eyebrows in return. "He shipped back in. In more than one way."

"Janey!" Claire scolded.

"I know, I know." Her friend didn't look abashed at all. "But, Claire, he was so tan and buff—and eager, after a year in the desert. Social opportunities there are mighty limited."

"So you took pity on a poor, lonely marine."

"Believe me, I got as much as I gave." Her friend got a quizzical look on her face. "I wonder if your Green Beret is fresh from the sandbox."

"Sandbox?"

"What the soldiers call their Middle East deployments."

Claire shrugged. "I don't know, and I don't care. Whoever he is, he's probably some suck-up who thinks he can advance his career by doing a favor for a congressman."

"If Sergeant First Class…you said Boudreaux, right? If SFC Boudreaux was an ambitious suck-up, he sure wouldn't be in the Green Berets. Used to be Special Forces was a dead end on the army career ladder. Not so much anymore, but these guys are not your loudmouth glory hounds who go overseas with their general on fact-finding missions and brag how they heard gunfire from five miles away." Janey frowned. "Man, I wanna go overseas. Riding a desk in D.C. is not what I had in mind when I joined the army."

"I wish Sergeant Boudreaux would go back." Claire knew she was probably pouting but didn't care.

"He's probably not any happier to do this than you

are." Janey did lunges to stretch her calf muscles. "He's either missing out on team training time or personal leave. Instead of hanging out in the woods, doing mock warfare with his buddies, or even better, getting laid and drunk, he's got to train some squeamish chick who once spent two hours looking for her convertible in the Tysons Galleria parking lot."

"So I'm directionally challenged—I came out the Macy's door instead of Neiman Marcus," Claire mumbled.

"Claire, your dad had dropped you off that day—you didn't even have your car."

"All right, Janey, all right." Claire's face flushed. "Maybe I do need to reinforce some outdoor skills."

Janey nodded and smiled encouragingly. "I'm sure you'll learn a lot of useful things from Sergeant First Class Boudreaux."

Claire knew her friend was worried about her being able to take care of herself, but at least Janey wasn't haranguing her like her dad. Once she got back from San Lucas, it was time to get her own place.

"We'd better move before we cramp up." Janey took off jogging backward, her face mischievous. "Here's a new cadence especially for you. 'I wanna be a Green Beret.'"

"I wanna…be a…Green Beret." Claire was starting to puff again.

"'Live the life of sex and foreplay….'"

"Janey!"

2

"READY TO GET UP AND at 'em?" Her father's falsely hearty voice boomed through the large conference room at Ft. Bragg, North Carolina. A gleaming wood table dominated the room with photos of base commanders and world maps framed on the walls. He gestured at one of his aides to set Claire's gear under a white dry-erase board. Claire was scheduled to start her training the next day, but her father had insisted on a meet-and-greet with her trainer before sending her off, and the commanding officer had wanted to inspect her gear. "Learn all about the great outdoors, eh, kitten?"

"Dad, please," Claire muttered. Bad enough she looked like some tricked-out Victorian explorer with seventeen pockets on her super-expensive, brand-new, quick-dry khaki vest and cargo pants. Bad enough she was like Jane about to meet her own personal ape-man. Bad enough she was twenty-four and was still called "kitten."

She tried to ignore her dad and her churning stomach, in that order, and focused on a large painted wooden logo on the wall. Black and silver, the words *De Oppresso Liber* were painted in a semicircle under a six-pronged star. She walked closer—the star was actually a pair of crossed arrows over a long, lethal-looking knife.

According to what Claire had found out searching online after her run with Janey, the Green Berets didn't need any arrows or knives. They could probably kill somebody with a paper clip and a plastic drinking straw—the bendy kind.

De Oppresso Liber. She guessed from her French and Spanish classes that the Latin motto meant From Oppression Freeing or something like that. Freedom from oppression. A noble goal.

In her own little way, that was Claire's goal, too. Not that anyone would consider her oppressed. After all, her father was one of the most powerful politicians in America, her family had plenty of money and she had never wondered if she would have enough to eat. Nothing to complain about, yet…

She wasn't truly free because she hadn't tried to be. No Declaration of Independence had flowed from her pen, no charge up San Juan Hill, no stand at the Alamo. Well, maybe not that last one—she had cried when she visited the mission-fort in San Antonio and seen where real heroes had given their lives for their beliefs.

But it had always been easier to go along with her dad's plans for her, especially after her mother died, when they had clung to each other in their grief.

Claire snuck a look at her father, who was giving a long list of instructions to his assistant. Her father had moved on, had even casually dated a few widows or divorcées. She was actually okay with that, knowing that he would always cherish the love he had for her mother. He had a good and full life, but Claire? Not so much.

Clinging time was over for Claire Cook, the Human Kudzu Vine. Her turning point had come six months ago on the second anniversary of her mother's death, when she had steeled herself to look through the family photo albums her father had shoved to the back of the library closet.

Her mother had been the antithesis of "cling," especially in the black-and-white photos of her as a young girl and then the faded color pictures of her as a teenager—always in the settlement or the jungle surrounding it. The only difference between her and the local girls was lighter skin and more clothing, on the insistence of her parents.

Claire moved along the wall to look at several photos of the base, as well as photos of men in green or tan uniforms. Each one's face was carefully turned away from the camera or otherwise indistinguishable on film. Men building shelters, carrying weapons, reading maps. Men who had no doubt about who they were and what they were meant to do.

Seeing her mother's joyful face and remembering the stories and struggles of their lives in San Lucas,

Claire had carefully closed the album and written her grandfather's successor, Dr. Schmidt.

Her father's droning voice had stopped, and a new electric current ran through the room. She turned away from the wall. Three men stood inside the doorway, the older one some kind of commanding officer and the younger two his subordinates.

Her father leaped to his feet and gave the officer a hearty handshake. "Ah, Colonel Spencer, we spoke on the phone. A pleasure to finally meet you in person."

"Congressman. Ma'am." The colonel gave her a curt nod. Claire nodded in return, noting he didn't verbalize his own delight. The colonel looked like a tougher twin of her father, his silver hair clipped close instead of styled, his green cammies neatly pressed.

If the colonel was spic-and-span army, his men looked like they belonged in the army jail. Were soldiers even allowed to wear beards? The taller, blond guy looked like he might be the cheerful type on a good day, but obviously today wasn't a good day. He, on the other hand, looked like Miss Susie Sunshine compared to his companion. Claire had a nasty feeling that the darker man more closely resembled a man named Luc Boudreaux than Blondie did.

Blackbeard in the flesh. His eyes were two pieces of black coal, cold and glittering. His hair waved well past his collar, his beard covering most of his tanned face. He looked as if he hadn't shaved in months.

Janey's words about being fresh from the sandbox popped into Claire's head. Fresh from the desert to the swamp. No wonder he looked ready to spit nails.

Colonel Spencer gestured to his men. "Congressman Cook, Miss Cook, I'd like you to meet Captain Magnus Olson and Sergeant First Class Luc Boudreaux. Captain Olson has kindly released Sergeant Boudreaux from his current duties to serve as your trainer."

Their lips tightened briefly under all the facial hair. How much pressure had her father exerted on them? They certainly didn't look like eager volunteers.

A knock sounded at the door. Claire gasped. "Janey, what are you doing here?" Her friend stood in her dress uniform, her hat under her arm.

Janey wouldn't meet her eyes and snapped a perfect salute to Colonel Spencer and Captain Olson. The colonel returned it and the captain waved his hand vaguely toward his eyebrow. "First Lieutenant Jane Merrick reporting for duty, sir."

"At ease, Lieutenant." He took the packet of papers Janey offered him and scanned through the sheets, a cynical smile spreading over his face.

"Duty?" Claire asked. As far as she knew, Janey's Pentagon stint was to last at least another six to eight months. Why would they send her to Ft. Bragg? "Are you here on account of me?"

"Sir, my commanding officer ordered me to report to Fort Bragg as a special liaison between his office and yours." Janey still refused to look at Claire, but the tips of her ears were turning red. Captain Olson and Sergeant Boudreaux didn't change expression but Claire sensed their disgust.

"Well, well." Colonel Spencer slapped her papers against his open palm. "An unexpected present from our brethren—and sisters—in arms at the Pentagon. My memory is a tad faulty—are we conducting some joint operation that requires a liaison?"

"Sir, I don't know. I am just following my orders." Janey looked miserable but didn't back down.

The colonel sighed. "Yes, I expect you are." He turned to Claire. "Miss Cook, I assume you know the lieutenant?"

"Yes, we were roommates at UVA—University of Virginia. Go Cavaliers," she finished weakly.

"I was a West Point man myself. Congressman Cook?" He turned to her father.

"Colonel," her father said brightly.

"I don't suppose you would know why First Lieutenant Merrick was plucked from her important desk job in our nation's military command center and sent down to pal around with us lowly Special Forces types, would you?"

"A chaperone." Claire jumped to hear the sergeant's clipped Cajun tones. "Congressman Cook got himself a chaperone for his li'l girl."

Her father's mouth twitched guiltily. Claire wanted to die a thousand deaths. "Oh, Janey, I am so sorry he dragged you into this. Dad, how could you? Janey doesn't deserve this."

"Yo' *papa* don't trust you're alone in the woods with a big, bad Green Beret?" For the first time, Sergeant Boudreaux met her shamed gaze with a mocking one of his own. "You must be quite the tiger."

"Shut your mouth, you!" Her father shot to his feet, his face mottled.

"No offense, sir, but you're not my commanding officer, and last I checked, Fort Bragg is still in the U.S. of A., where freedom of speech still applies."

"Zip it, Boudreaux," his captain said without heat.

"Zipping it, sir." He closed his mouth, his point made.

"No, you zip it, Dad!" Claire turned on her father. "That man is totally justified in his outrage."

"Outrage," Boudreaux mused. "Now that is a *fine* word for this situation."

"You zip it, too! I'm trying to defend you here," Claire cried in frustration.

He arched a black eyebrow at her. "*Bébé,* do I look like a man who needs defending?"

She huffed out a breath and turned back to her father. "You have constantly thrown up roadblocks to my plans, you have tampered with the workings of the U.S. Army, and meddled with the careers of Janey and at least three of her fellow soldiers. You've abused your authority and are a disgrace to your office."

"I don't know about that, *cher,*" Boudreaux interjected with a smirk. "Your daddy hasn't been indicted,

served prison time or accidentally killed someone—
he's an amateur in comparison to his fellow politicians."

Captain Olson unsuccessfully muffled a snort. Colonel Spencer intently studied the ceiling, his jaw twitch-
ing.

Claire clenched her trembling fists. "Dad, I have had
enough. I am going to San Lucas, Janey is going to
Washington and these nice men can go wherever they
had planned to go before you came along. Hopefully to
a barber," she added, ticked off at the sergeant's enjoy-
ment of her embarrassment. And who was he to call her
cher, anyway, in that mocking French-tinged accent?

She hurried from the conference room, ignoring her
father's shouts, wanting to escape. She dashed into the
humid Carolina afternoon, crossing the parking lot into
a small landscaped grove with a picnic bench. The scent
of pines didn't quite cover the smell of diesel and something else pungent—explosives? She wasn't sure. Claire
climbed onto the picnic table, her feet resting on the
bench.

A new scent came along, clean and masculine. She
turned and stifled a yelp. Good thing Sergeant
Boudreau was wearing cologne because she certainly
hadn't heard him approach. Of course, that would be
a plus in his line of work. He stood next to her and
stared across the parking lot, shoving his hands into
the back pockets of his jeans, tightening the thin fabric
across his zipper. Not that she noticed things like that.

"Don't worry—you're off the hook." Claire didn't want to meet his mocking glance again. "I'll be fine— the Río San Lucas settlement is like a small town, running water and everything so I can wash my hair." She gave a little laugh, trying to get him to leave her alone.

"Why you wanna go down to that jungle snake hole anyway, Mademoiselle Cook?" This time he wasn't mocking, just curious. "You got somethin' to prove to your *papa?*"

She tried to hide her flinch. "Maybe I have something to prove to myself."

"There are easier ways to do that. Go mountain climbing or white-water rafting if you want to see how tough you are. Walk across the country to raise money for cancer, but moving to the jungle doesn't make you tough—just foolish."

Claire saw red. "Shut up! You denigrate my mother, my grandmother and my grandfather." She slammed her fist into her palm as she named each of her family members. "They moved to San Lucas to serve people who had no one and had nothing. You talk to all the women who lived after my grandfather saved them during difficult childbirth—you talk to all their babies who lived because they had their mothers to breast-feed them. You ask them how foolish it is that they are alive and not buried in an unmarked jungle grave site!"

He stood in silence for a minute. "I apologize," he finally said.

Claire almost fell off the picnic table. "What?"

He ran a strong hand through his wavy hair. "I have been extremely rude and my *grand-mère* and *maman* would pass me a slap. My only defense is that I've been overseas away from civilization too long."

"How long?" she asked without thinking.

"Now that's classified information, ma'am."

His scornful attitude was back. "I'd say at least seven or eight months according to your facial hair," she retorted. "If you don't want people speculating, the least you could do is get a haircut and shave." He did look good as a pirate—maybe he was descended from Jean Lafitte, the famous Louisianan pirate.

"Maybe you should sign up as an intelligence agent instead. It was actually eight months and ten days." He rubbed his chin.

"Claire! Claire!" Her father's voice echoed out the main door of the office building.

She pressed her lips together. She was definitely getting her own place, San Lucas or no. Dad had gone too far.

"There you are, Claire." He hurried up to her, ignoring Boudreaux. "Now can you see how foolish this idea of yours is?" he asked, unknowingly echoing Boudreaux's earlier taunt.

Next to her, the Green Beret sucked in a breath, obviously waiting for her to lose her temper with her father like she had with him.

But her will had been tempered into steel. "Who's going to look like the bigger fool at the press conference I'll arrange—me, for wanting to go to San Lucas, or you, for throwing so many inappropriate roadblocks into my path? Now you're interfering with the U.S. Army."

"And during an election year, too," Boudreaux added helpfully. "Sir."

"You'd do that? To your own father?" He was practically stammering in indignation.

"You were always talking about retiring."

"Retiring! Retiring, not losing to that nobody state senator who's running against me."

"If your constituents don't like your little forays into meddling, they can vote their opinion. I may endorse your opponent myself," she added darkly.

Her father made a choking noise, but wasn't turning any funny colors or clutching his chest so Claire figured he was only pissed off.

She turned to the sergeant. "So you're off the hook with me. Again, I'm sorry for this mess, and I'll make sure it doesn't harm you or your career."

He stared silently at her, his dark eyes unreadable.

She fumbled slightly but finally shoved her hands into two of the pants' eight pockets.

Her father finally found his voice. "You ungrateful child!" He swung around and stomped off to where his aide stood back at the building practically wringing his hands.

"The man surely has a sense of the dramatic. I'm shocked he didn't quote *King Lear* at you."

"What?" Claire looked at him in surprise.

"I see you as more of a Cordelia type—the dutiful daughter who is the only one to stick with her cranky old dad."

Claire blinked. "Yes, I read *King Lear* in college. When did you read it?"

"The army sends Shakespeare comic books overseas for us to look at the pictures when we aren't blowing things up." He delivered his smarty-pants answer with a straight face.

"Oh, buzz off!" She jumped off the picnic table, intending to find Janey and beg her forgiveness.

Boudreaux blocked her way so quickly she didn't see him move. "I'll do it."

"Do what?" Claire turned to him.

"Train you. Get ready for San Lucas—as ready as you can be. As ready as anyone can be," he muttered to himself.

"You will?" Claire's heart beat faster.

"I'll tell you right now—you're nuts for wanting to go, and I fully plan on making you rethink your decision." Her stomach flipped at the first smile she'd seen from him, his teeth flashing white in his black beard. "In fact, I plan on making you *regret* your decision."

OLIE RUBBED HIS BARE chin, which was fish-belly pale in comparison to his sun-darkened cheekbones and forehead. He had dragged Luc off to the base's barber shop, as well, yesterday after the colonel had yelled at them a new one for looking scruffy, especially in front of so-called VIPs. "Rage, you said she spiked her old man's guns so he can't cause trouble for us. We're all off the hook—so why are you doing this?" He gestured to the bartender for a couple beers as they sat side-by-side in the Special Forces' local hangout.

Luc shook his head, his hair now too short to brush his collar. "I'm gonna try like hell to convince her to give up this dumb idea. But if I can't, the girl's gonna go, whether she knows jack-shit about the jungle or not. How will I feel four, five months from now if I hear she got snakebit, got herself sick eating something she shouldn't have, or worse, gets herself out in the jungle and doesn't come back?"

"Been known to happen." Olie nodded solemnly. The bartender set down their drinks.

"That it has." Luc nodded back. They had lost a teammate in the same incident that had stranded Luc for five weeks. Luc knew it still ate up Olie, him being the commanding officer and all, even if it wasn't his fault. Luc lifted his mug in a silent toast to fallen brothers in arms. Olie lifted his in reply and they both drank solemnly.

After a few minutes, Olie broke the silence.

"As long as that's all you do with her."

"What's that supposed to mean?"

"Miss Cook is not exactly hard on the eyes, Rage. Pretty hair, bright smile and a sweet disposition all look mighty nice to a man who hasn't got laid for almost nine months. Maybe you should reconsider and take that cute lieutenant with you after all."

Luc straightened in outrage. "You saying she's not safe with me? That I need a chaperone to make sure I act as a gentleman and a soldier of the United States Army?"

"At ease." Olie waved a hand at him. "All I'm saying is that a ragin' Cajun, war hero-type like yourself might appeal to a girl who's finally away from her overprotective dad. Too much of that Frenchie accent and she may go crazy and throw herself at you."

"Right," Luc scoffed. "Princess Cook probably has some weenie boyfriend named Preston Shelby Blueblood the Nineteenth waiting for her back in ol' Virginia. He'll spend the next year screwing around on her while she's in San Lucas and ask her to marry him as soon as she gets off the plane. They'll have a couple kids while he keeps screwing around on her and dumps her for his secretary in ten years." He subsided into a funk, realizing he sounded like an idiot.

"O-kay." Olie raised his blond eyebrows. "Well, our immediate concern is not for her future marital happiness, so that's one burden we don't have to carry."

"Yes, sir," Luc muttered. What the hell was wrong with him? Her personal life was none of his damn business anyway.

Olie's cell phone rang and he flipped it open, answering with several "yes, sirs." He closed the phone and swiveled on the bar stool back to Luc. "Colonel Spencer says he made arrangements for you both with the marines at Parris Island. The swamp is about as close to jungle as you can get in the Southeast."

Luc wished he could take her back to Louisiana, but everything was still torn up from the hurricane last fall, and he didn't think he could stand being so close to home and not see his family. And he wasn't about to come home with a woman. His mother would never understand his unorthodox situation and would be calling Father Andre at the church to set a wedding date. He shuddered.

Olie continued, "She'll do her training during the day and sleep in the VIP quarters at night."

"Shit, they don't even want her to know how to make shelter at night? That's where you run in to trouble."

Olie grunted. "She probably gets her bed turned down and a mint on her pillow." He dug around in the nut dish and chose a big brown Brazil nut.

"Funny, I don't remember mints on my pillow when I was in the jungle—the only brown things under my head were bugs. And at one point, that bug *was* my bedtime snack." Luc ate a peanut. *Pistaches de terre,* they called them at home. Too salty—he liked plain boiled peanuts better.

Olie shook his head. "Not doing her any favors by letting her off easy at night."

Luc thought for several seconds. Nuts to the jarheads at Parris Island and their VIP quarters. Survival training without night training meant no survival at all. "This thing with Claire Cook is still an unofficial thing—I'm on leave as of now, right?"

"Yeah. Why?" Olie gave him a wary look, his fingers clamped around a cashew.

"Just want to make sure I'm not going AWOL if I take her on a side trip."

Olie dropped the cashew. "AWOL? Side trip?" He covered his ears with his beefy hands and shook his head. "As far as I'm concerned, the only side trip I need to know about is to the Parris Island ice cream stand."

Luc set down his empty mug. He knew just the place he would take her. One of his old buddies had bought a huge chunk of land abutting a national wildlife refuge and had invited Luc and the guys to use it whenever he wanted. It was really out in the middle of nowhere. The animals couldn't yet read the signs telling them they were leaving federal land, so plenty wound up at his friend's place. No marines, no babysitters, no chaperones. Him, her and the swamp.

People who weren't used to the swamp freaked out pretty easily at all the weird noises, smells and bugs. Maybe if they were lucky, he'd even take her out at night when the gators roared. "We'll be out in the swamp twenty-four, thirty-six hours tops before she starts crying to go home to Daddy."

"You think so, huh." His CO shook his head. "We'll see, Rage. We'll see."

3

A TAP SOUNDED ON CLAIRE'S hotel room door. She looked up from the San Lucas guidebook she had been reading and tucked a bookmark inside.

She hadn't ordered room service, and her father was still probably drinking bourbon and smoking illicit Cuban cigars at the hotel's private men's club with the esteemed senator for the state of North Carolina. She hopped out of bed and peeked through the peephole.

A black-haired stranger stood in front of her door, his face turned to the side. Wow, was he a looker with a strong, clean jaw and firm, full lips. His short haircut indicated that he was probably military despite the fact he wore jeans and a black T-shirt. What should she do? It was past midnight. "Yes?" she ventured, tugging her peach-colored cotton robe around her.

"Miss Cook?" He stopped scanning the hall and stared at the peephole.

She swallowed hard. "Sergeant Boudreaux?" she asked faintly. Good Lord, the man cleaned up well. Better than well, magnificently.

"You alone, ma'am?"

"Of course." She undid the chain and yanked open the door. "Who else would be here with me?" As if she'd brought a boyfriend when she had important preparation to do.

He gave her an amused smile. "Oh, I don't know—maybe your father or your friend the lieutenant."

"Oh." Her mind had immediately jumped to things of a sexual nature and she blamed *him*. Worst of all, he knew what she'd assumed.

"If you're not comfortable letting me into your room, we can meet downstairs in the bar."

"No, no, that's all right." She stopped clutching the door and opened it for him. "Come in."

"Thank you, ma'am." He stepped into her room and looked around. "Never been in this hotel before even though it's not too far from the base. Fancy."

Claire supposed it was, with its high ceilings designed for hot Southern nights, creamy warm yellow wallpaper and matching bedding. She snuck a glance at the dark wooden four-poster bed behind her, which seemed to have tripled in size since she'd answered the door.

His gaze followed hers. "Nice bed."

"Um, yes. Yes, it is, although I haven't really tried it out yet. Since we just got here today." She'd been too nervous to sleep, knowing she'd be out in the woods with him tomorrow, but that was nothing compared to having him in her bedroom. "You got a shave and a haircut." She couldn't think of anything else to say.

"You suggested it, didn't you?" He rubbed his chin. "Feels strange to have a smooth face after so many months."

Claire never guessed he was so handsome under all that hair. She couldn't stop watching his hand rub his tight, tanned skin. Her nipples tightened and she gathered her robe closer. "What brings you here, Sergeant?"

"You."

"What?"

"I need to make sure you're ready."

Oh, she was. But probably not for what he had in mind. "I'll be at the base at oh-seven-hundred hours like we planned." She thought her little foray into military time was pretty good, but he obviously disagreed.

"Real training should start at what we call 'oh-dark-thirty.'"

"What time is that?" It sounded terribly early.

"Whenever the CO hauls your ass out of bed— three, four o'clock in the morning."

"My goodness, that is early."

"The old army recruiting slogan had it right—'we do more before 9:00 a.m. than most people do all day.'"

"Shouldn't they have said 'oh-nine-hundred'?" He gave her a strange look. "I mean, using military time and all that…"

"Let me see your stuff." Without getting permission, Sergeant Boudreaux hefted one duffel bag. "Crap! Can you even lift this thing?" He easily tossed it to Claire, but its weight pitched her backward onto the bed and she found herself staring at the underside of the yellow canopy.

He muttered another curse and pulled the bag off her chest. "You okay?"

She nodded as she tried to catch her breath. Before she knew it, he was kneeling next to her on the bed and running his hands expertly over her shoulders and arms. He hesitated briefly as his fingers brushed the sides of her unbound breasts, but continued his check-up. "Take a deep breath."

Claire did, her robe falling open to reveal her sheer cotton nightgown. His gaze fell to the rise and fall of her breasts, and she realized the dark circles of her nipples were visible.

Boudreaux swallowed. "Does it hurt?" His voice was thick and sweet as cane syrup.

"Does *what* hurt?" Her nipples were starting to hurt from being so hard. Despite his rough exterior, his hands had been gentle.

"Your chest. I mean, when you breathe." His own breath was coming faster.

"You mean, here?" Some little devil made Claire massage the tops of her breasts and breastbone between.

His hands clearly gripped his jeans-clad knees. "Yeah. There. Do I need to call you an ambulance?"

She stopped, disappointed. "No. Are you trying to break my ribs so I don't go?"

He leaped off the bed so smoothly the only evidence he'd ever been there was his imprint on the duvet. "Back to the duffel." He crouched and unzipped it while she sat up. "Camping gear?" He lifted a sarcastic eyebrow. "What did you do, clean out the Bass Pro Shop?"

"No, of course not!" It had been the L.L. Bean catalog.

He pulled out each item, giving a running tally. "Sleeping bag, sleeping bag *pillow,* mess kit, ground sheet—okay, that might be useful…biodegradable dish soap?" He shook his head. "Planning on doing any dishes? A GPS unit—do you even know how to use this? Got any extra batteries? They go bad quickly in hot, damp climates. Oh, look, how useful. An unsharpened pocketknife. Got a whetstone?"

Claire shrugged. She wasn't sure.

Boudreaux continued, "No compass, no whetstone, no machete—"

"Machete? What's that for?"

"A machete, or ma-chay-tay, as our Spanish-speaking friends would call it, is *the* golden ticket to survival. You wanna make friends in the Amazon, you bring the natives high-quality machetes, and lots of them. If you've never seen the gardener on your family estate use one, they look like a really big knife curved on the sharp side."

Claire curled her lip at the crack about her "family estate." "Where do I get a machete?"

"I have several. You can borrow one for now."

She was already bringing medical supplies for the hospital and educational supplies for the school, but she'd have to talk to Dr. Schmidt about how to bring machetes. She didn't suppose she could throw several foot-long knives into her airline carry-on.

"And your other bag?" He lifted the smaller duffel bag. "Don't worry. Now that I know you have no upper-body strength I won't throw this at you."

"It's a bit late for developing upper-body strength, don't you think?"

He gave her an evil grin. "It's never too late for push-ups. And no girl push-ups, either, where your butt's sticking up in the air."

"You want me to drop and give you twenty? That way you can check how my butt is." She challenged him with her hands on her hips, knowing her loose nightgown would gape all the way down to her toes.

He noticed the same thing and backpedaled. "Maybe later." He crouched and unzipped the smaller bag. "Ah, clothes from the discount rank-amateur-survivalist collection."

"I did not shop discount," she informed him. He held up a khaki shirt.

"Not bad—quick drying. But four of them? And one's pink? No way I am going into the swamp with you wearing pink. Never hear the end of it." He dug around further. "Six t-shirts, three pairs shorts, three pairs hiking pants. A packable poncho—good for making shelter. What looks like seventeen pairs of socks."

"I blister easily."

He gave her an incredulous look. "You kidding me? Bad feet in the jungle? What, you wanna get jungle rot or blood poisoning from a bad blister?"

"They're special socks," she informed him.

"Mon Dieu." He shook his head. "Special socks. I'm beginning to sympathize with your father more and more, Claire."

It was the first time he'd used her first name, but she figured they'd moved past a certain formality when he'd run his hands near her breasts and stared at her nipples. She liked the way he said it in his French accent, the *R* at the end a little purring noise.

She was too busy mooning over that to notice he'd moved on to the deepest corner of her bag. "Hey!"

He had a fistful each of her bras and panties and was examining them with a clinical eye. Of course it wasn't any of her delicate, lacy things she had a secret weakness for—these were industrial-strength white or gray cotton sports bras and panties.

"Put those back, those are none of your business." She grabbed for them, but of course he was too quick.

"Everything about you is my business now, down to your underwear." He stuffed them into the bag. "Glad to see you brought one hundred percent cotton. Prickly heat and fungal infections are no joke."

Claire winced but he had moved on to the hiking boots she'd left next to the door. He examined the specially vented sides designed to drain water and sweat, tested the soles' flexibility and tugged on the laces. He stopped and examined one lace closely.

"Is it getting frayed?" She hoped not. She had gone online and researched her boots, knowing her feet would be her weak point. These were supposed to be the best jungle-trekking boots made.

Boudreaux unlaced one boot. She probably hadn't laced it up to Green Beret requirements. He straightened, his face serious, the boot dangling from his hand. "What do you know about the plans your father has made for your training?"

"Oh, um, he said we would all drive down to Parris Island tomorrow and get started. I'm not sure how far that is."

"It's about two hundred and fifty miles. Ever been there?"

She shook her head.

"It's the Marine Corps recruiting depot for the eastern United States. Big installation. The feds do their outdoor training there." He eyed her closely. "Your father made reservations for the two of you to stay in the VIP quarters at night after you train with me during the day."

"So we would go out into the woods for the day and come back every night?" It sounded cushy to Claire, but not particularly effective.

"You didn't know about your hotel arrangements?"

"I figured we'd pitch a couple of pup tents so I could learn how."

"Pup tents. Right." He held up her boot. "Did you realize you have a tracking device here?"

"A what?"

"Somebody planted what looks like a GPS tracking device on the tongue of your boot. See this black disc? Your other boot doesn't have it."

Claire stared at the plastic circle. "I barely noticed that—I thought it was an antitheft device from the store."

"It is. An antitheft device for *you.* Not your boot. Whoever planted this can log in to a GPS server and find exactly where your boot is, every minute of every day."

"Who would want to…" Claire's question trailed away. Of course she knew who wanted to track her— her father. Good grief, she'd seen ads for things like this, but to find lost children who'd wandered away at the playground, not keep tabs on a grown adult. Then a worse thought hit her. Had her father put trackers in her car, her purse?

She ran across the room and dumped her purse on the bed. "Check out my stuff. I need to know if I have any more electronic babysitters."

Boudreaux methodically examined every thing she normally carried with her. Claire blushed briefly when he found the little pouch that held her tampons and a couple condoms she'd forgotten about. His black gaze flicked to her face but he didn't change his expression.

He probed the lining of her purse and stopped. "Here." He pulled out a razor-sharp-looking pocket-knife and slit a seam before working something out with his fingers.

She leaned over his shoulder. "Another one," she said dully. It was a match to the one on her shoe.

"Want me to check your duffel bags?"

"No." She waved off his offer, slumping onto the bed, her shoulders hunching.

"You think it's your father?"

"Who else?"

"Disgruntled boyfriend? Someone who's unhappy you're leaving him for so long?" He looked down at her in concern.

She let out a decidedly unladylike snort. "Not hardly. I haven't even had sex in almost a year." She slapped a hand over her mouth. Great. Now she sounded like some sort of desperate weirdo.

He bit back a smile. "If it makes you feel better, neither have I."

Instead of clearing the air, their mutual admission of celibacy thickened it. The condoms on her bed beckoned. Condoms, bed and extended celibacy were a potent combination.

Who would need to know if she made a move on him? She was leaving for San Lucas in less than a month, where the sexual opportunities were probably slim. She'd never been so bold with a total stranger, but he had shown her flashes of gentleness under his tough exterior. "Luc." His name was strange and wonderful on her tongue as she ran her hand up his muscled forearm to where his bicep met his soft cotton T-shirt.

He stood frozen as a statue, the only movement in his body under his tight zipper. Emboldened, she brushed her palm over his rock-hard pec, his nipple responding instantly. He closed his eyes and shuddered.

"Luc, you feel—"

"Dammit!" His eyes flew open and he caught her wrist.

"What?"

"I feel *too* good, that's what. And you'd feel too good under me." He shoved her hand away from him. "And *this* is why women are not allowed in Special Forces. Your skin is too smooth, your body is too soft—hell, even that sweet peachy smell coming off your hair is a dangerous distraction."

"You think I'm a distraction?" Despite his rejection and backhanded compliments, she was pleased.

"I know so." He pointed a finger at her. "And you don't need any distractions, either. I will not be hanging around the jungles of San Lucas de la Selva ready to rescue you with my machete in my hand and my knife between my teeth. The only person you can depend on is *you.*"

"How sad."

"What?"

"Don't you depend on your family? Your team?"

"Family will not get you out of a jam if you're far away, and your team, well…" He looked away for a second. "Sometimes your team is gone and it's just you."

"Oh."

He stared at her. "If you don't want to do this, back out. But if you want to have at least a fighting chance of taking care of yourself, come with me now."

"Now?" she squeaked. It was almost one in the morning.

"*Oui,* now. That Parris Island training is bullshit. You can't learn anything if you know you've got a hot shower and fluffy bed waiting for you at the end of the day. And don't forget, your *papa's* going to hover over you with his little GPS tracker to make sure you don't get lost—a real eye in the sky."

Claire's lips tightened. In the heat of touching Luc, she'd almost forgotten about that sneaky trick. "What do I need to do?"

"Do everything I tell you." He pulled out a clean outfit for her and checked every item. "No tracking devices in the things. Get dressed."

"Okay." Some impish impulse made her shrug off her robe and stand before him in just her nightgown. He stared at her, his eyes dark and hungry. She started to push one strap off her shoulder when he snapped out of it.

"You, go in the bathroom, you. I'm going to my truck for a bag to pack your stuff." He hurried out, checking the hall before he left.

He wanted her, she could tell. But discipline was winning over desire.

LUC RUSHED TO HIS TRUCK, his muscles practically quivering from the effort to restrain himself from showing Miss Claire Cook how nice that big bed could be. He leaned his forehead against the frame of his red truck. He was totally crazy in the head, to think going out alone into the field with this woman was a good idea.

Hell, he was totally nuts to have turned her down. Sweet Mam'zelle Claire had practically thrown herself at him, condoms at the ready, and what had he done?

Turned her down. Turned down a sweet-smelling, shiny-haired, pretty lady with full, plump breasts and dark, shadowy nipples that had poked out like his cock when he touched her.

He cursed again. If only he'd had even a few days to go out, have a couple beers, meet some good-looking chicks who were interested in checking out his battle scars in close, personal detail. Maybe the top of his head wouldn't be about to blow off.

The guys on his team with girlfriends or wives didn't have this problem. They'd all disappeared into their bedrooms and didn't come up for air for at least a week.

But no girlfriend or wife for Luc. He'd seen too many relationships wrecked by Special Forces deployments, seen too many of his teammates dumped via e-mail or satellite phone. Green Berets weren't supposed to cry but he'd seen his teammates break down. Living in some cave ten thousand miles away from everyone you loved gave a "Dear John" knife in the back an extra-deep twist.

Luc wasn't so smug in his current situation, though. He rubbed his sweaty forehead with his sleeve. He needed to get himself under control or else he'd be making his way through the swamp with his pecker pointing the way.

"WHERE ARE WE GOING?" Claire was shouting since Luc had slipped in a CD of loud rock music. It was probably a good thing she couldn't understand more than a third of the lyrics. The green dashboard lights showed Luc's hard, set expression as he tapped his truck's steering wheel in time to the beat.

"South."

"Oh." They had left the main road several miles ago and were passing small towns, their lights darkened for the night. "I should call somebody to let them know our plans." She would need to use his phone, since hers had sported a tracking device, as well.

Luc lowered the stereo volume slightly. "You left two voice mails and a note for your father. I think he'll be okay. Pissed off, but okay."

"Yes, I know." Claire twisted her fingers as she looked around the truck's interior. She'd practically needed a ladder to climb into it, but the interior was almost as luxurious as her dad's Euro luxury car—soft leather seats, totally digital controls, a smooth ride. Only her father's German car didn't have a gun rack in the back window.

"Where are your guns?" she asked.

"Why you want to know? You gonna shoot me?"

"No, of course not." She was aghast.

"You might by the time we're done." He grinned. "I have a sidearm, a rifle and a shotgun in my bags. All properly unloaded and broken down, of course." He shot her a look. "You know how to use any of those?"

"Uh, some target shooting. Oh, and my dad took me skeet shooting once but I wasn't very good at it. The reporters kept distracting me."

"Election year, huh?"

"Every year is election year when you're a U.S. Representative." How many times had Claire and her mother been trotted out at a campaign event? "If it's not an actual voting year, it's a fund-raising year. My mother did most of the events until I got out of high school, and then she took a job teaching anthropology at the local college and I volunteered to do more."

"Wasn't your job to do his work for him, Claire."

"Public events always look better with family members." That was what her father had said.

"Especially if the family members are photogenic young women. Hope you didn't miss anything important."

"Not much. A couple sorority dances, an honor society induction, a semester in Paris that happened to be the fall term of an election year."

"A semester in Paris?" He gave a low whistle. "After all, how are you going to keep the girl on the Virginia farm, once she's seen Paris?"

"All right, that one still bothers me. I studied French for seven years and never even studied anywhere French-speaking. It was too late to even make arrangements to go to Montreal."

"You can practice your French on me anytime. Course, Cajun French is over three hundred years old, so you may sound a bit out-of-date."

"Really? I did read that in one of my French classes, but our teacher was Parisian and all she would say is that it sounds strange. Then she sneered a bit."

"Yeah, well, we Cajuns are the linguistic hillbillies of the Francophone world."

Claire burst out laughing. "Madame la Professeur always was a snob."

Luc grunted.

"Have you ever worked with French soldiers?"

He gave her an amused look. *"Peut-être."*

"Maybe? Oh, right, you can't say. Just like Janey. I'm sure she has lots of interesting stories to tell me but she can't because they're classified." The only story

Janey had told her recently was about her exploits with the sexually frustrated marine. If only Janey knew how close Claire had come to having an exploit of her own. But no, the darn man was determined to resist her. Rats.

"Loose lips still sink ships. Your friend is smart to keep her mouth closed."

"That's right, Janey will keep her mouth closed. Maybe I can call her really quickly to let her know what's going on." For some strange reason, Claire trusted Luc to keep her safe but she still wanted to talk to someone, anyone, before going into the deep, dark woods.

"Okay." Luc dug in the console and handed her a phone. "Use this one to call your friend, and then we have radio silence. No calls unless it's life or death." He turned down the rock music.

Claire dialed her friend's cell-phone number, hoping she wouldn't get mad that Claire woke her.

Janey answered. "Hello?" she shouted over a pulsing country music beat.

"Janey, it's Claire."

"Claire? Why aren't you asleep? Aren't you leaving at seven?"

"I'm too nervous to sleep." That part was true. "Where are you? I thought you were going to the Airborne Inn." Claire had invited Janey to stay with her but her friend had decided to check in to the base lodging.

"Captain Olson kindly offered to show me around Fayetteville and I took him up on it." Janey lowered her voice as much as she could, considering the loud music. "He went to the bar for some refills. Holy crap, Claire. He turned into some blond stud once all that hair was gone." Like any good army officer, Janey preferred clean-cut men. "I almost fainted dead away when I realized who he was. What about you? Why aren't you in bed getting ready for your big day tomorrow?"

"Well, 'my big day tomorrow' started tonight."

"What?"

"Sergeant Boudreaux came to my hotel room," Claire began.

"Claire!" Janey squealed. "Did he get a shave and haircut, too? I bet he's hot now."

Claire gave Luc a sidelong glance. *"Hot"* didn't even start to describe him. Tabasco-sauce hot was more like it.

"If he's in your hotel room, why are you bothering to call me? Can't you think of anything better to do? As soon as I can manage without looking slutty, I'm going to knock Olie down and lick him all over. Thank goodness he's not my commanding officer. I'd die from unrequited lust if he were."

"Janey…" Claire muttered. She did not need any more sexual images running through her brain. "We're getting an early start on the training. Sergeant Boudreaux is taking me to the training center tonight."

"Training center? You mean Parris Island?" Janey sounded confused.

Claire turned to Luc. "Um, not exactly."

"Oh, Olie's back. Olie, your boy Boudreaux picked up Claire tonight and they're heading to some training center that may or may not be Parris Island."

Claire heard a deep male voice rumble.

"Oh. Olie says he doesn't want to know a thing about what you and Boudreaux are up to. He says he wants plausible deniability."

"Plausible deniability?" Claire repeated.

Boudreaux guffawed. "Have your friend tell Olie we're eloping."

Claire covered the mouthpiece on the phone. "No, I will not have Janey tell him that!"

"Good psy ops, Claire. Psychological warfare. Your father will be so grateful we're not running off to get married that he won't care about his plans for Parris Island being ruined."

"No, Luc!"

Janey's voice sounded from the phone. "Claire, Claire, is he giving you trouble? Do you want me to come get you?"

For a second, Claire wanted to tell Janey yes, tell her to come rescue poor little Claire from the yucky bugs and slimy snakes and squishy things that were waiting to crawl up her leg and bite her. But she didn't. "No, Janey, I'll be fine. You and Olie have a good time, and please apologize on my behalf for everyone's inconvenience."

Janey grumbled. "You apologize too much. Now go kick some swamp butt and don't do anything I wouldn't do."

"Maybe I'll do exactly what you're going to do."

"What? Oh, Claire. In the swamp? You make sure to check your bedding before you crawl in, okay?"

"Okay." They said their goodbyes and Claire hung up. Janey was right to remind her. The only body Claire wanted to crawl into her bedding was Luc's.

4

"CLAIRE? WAKE UP, CLAIRE."

She bolted upright from the reclining truck seat. When had she fallen asleep? The sun peeped over the trees lining the bumpy country road. She wiped her mouth discreetly. No drool. Good. "Where are we?"

"Almost to our destination."

"Which is?" She levered the seat to an upright position and stared out the window. The terrain was flat, covered in tall pines common in sandy soil. They could have been almost anywhere in the Southeast.

He turned the truck into a nearly hidden driveway overgrown with thick shrubs. "My buddy's place. I made arrangements to use a corner of his land. He has so much, he'll never miss it."

"But where are we?" she persisted.

"Georgia or South Carolina, depending on what side of the Savannah River you cross."

"Oh." That wasn't really helpful. "Near the city of Savannah?" she asked hopefully. Savannah was a super-nice town, full of great restaurants and beautiful Southern antebellum mansions.

"No, not near Savannah, so don't get your hopes up." He obviously knew her line of thinking. "If you wanted comfort, you should have stayed home."

"Right." She forced a cheerful grin onto her face and grimaced as her stomach rumbled. "I'm going to eat breakfast real quick here." She reached into her bag for the box of granola bars she'd stashed away. "Want one?"

He looked at the box. "Honey s'mores with choco-chunks and minimarshmallows?" He sounded more astonished than appalled. "Is that supposed to be healthy?"

"No." She ripped open a wrapper and sunk her teeth into the gooey goodness, her speech muffled as she talked with her mouth full. Her father would be horrified. "Ish shupposed to be tashty."

"Ah, what the hell." He accepted one and grimaced as the bar stuck to his fingers. "It's the last snack you'll have until we're done."

The treat soured on her tongue. "Then I guess I better have another."

CLAIRE HAD ACTUALLY EATEN two more granola bars, and was beginning to heartily regret her decision as Luc gunned the small fishing boat's outboard motor. She didn't think it was possible to be seasick on a lake, but it *was* a rather large lake.

She concentrated on breathing deeply and focusing on the opposite shore, facing away from him. "It was nice of your friend to loan us his boat," she called.

"*Oui.*"

"Sorry he wasn't home so I could thank him. Is he on a hunting trip?"

Luc laughed. "No, he's in D.C. briefing the president today."

She turned to look at him and hastily swiveled away as her stomach jumped. "Aren't you the funny one. If you can't tell me things, say so. I'm used to security clearances, you know." His friend was probably at the local Piggly Wiggly stocking up on barbecue sauce and beer.

"No, Claire. He actually is in D.C. to brief the president. My friend is an expert on several Middle Eastern hotspots."

"Oh." Claire decided Luc was serious. "Maybe my father knows him."

"Maybe."

And that was the end of their conversation for several minutes. Claire slapped at several mosquitoes, glad she had put on plenty of organic citronella-based repellent. She probably smelled like the fuel in a tiki torch, but better than being bitten up. She also wore a packable sun hat with a floppy brim.

Behind her, Luc sat in silence, no humming under his breath, no whistling, not even a sigh now and again. If it wasn't for the fact the boat was still running smoothly and she hadn't heard a big splash, she might have thought he'd fallen overboard. Probably all his training. After all, it was a bad idea to go around whistling and sighing when you were trying to sneak up on people to kill them.

She shivered slightly. She'd thought about the pro-verbial "law of the jungle"—kill, or be killed. How many times had he been in that situation? She really hoped she never was. It was going to be bad enough that they would eat "off the land," as Luc had put it when he ripped the box of granola bars from her death grip and had tossed it into his truck.

Eating off the land conjured up all sorts of yucky images of her food sitting on the ground in the dirt. Kind of like when you dropped a really expensive piece of chocolate on the pool deck, but picked it up and ate it anyway…only much, much worse.

He slowed and turned the boat into a smaller creek off the main lake. The bugs were much thicker here, little gnats that buzzed around her eyes and mouth. The towering trees covered the waterway, big clumps of Spanish moss dangling from the long branches. "Hey, maybe we can use some Spanish moss for bedding."

"Not unless you like mites and bugs. Stuff's crawl-ing with them."

"Never mind." Her thoughts churned as she and Luc cruised through the water, weaving their way up smaller and smaller rivers, farther and farther from the lake's relative civilization. Oh, dear, what was she in for? The VIP quarters at Parris Island were looking mighty nice about now. "What's our first step?"

"You're not going to have nearly enough time to

prepare, so I need to get you up to speed on the basics. Swamp is different than jungle, but the closest we can get for now. All sorts of tricks you can learn except one."

That didn't sound good. "What?"

"Toughness." He overrode her protests about how she had been getting in shape for this for months. "None of that matters like mental toughness. How tough are you?"

"Probably not very," she admitted.

He cut the engine and they drifted through the greeny-brown water. "Turn around, Claire. We're going slow enough that you won't get motion sick."

She thought she'd hid that pretty good. She frowned quickly before smoothing her face and turning around. "Yes?"

The early morning sun threw some dappled rays onto his face. Claire stifled a gasp. With a short coating of stubble, he was even more handsome than last night.

"You have to pay attention to me, Claire, or you won't learn." He gave her a narrow stare before continuing. "Your mind is your biggest asset. I've seen big, muscular men reduced to tears 'cause they weren't strong-minded. You know who survives best in crappy situations?"

"The ones who know the most about the jungle, or wherever they get stranded."

"Wrong. The ones who want to live the most. Mothers, who are trying to get home to their children.

Fathers, who walk fifty miles through snow for help for their families. The soldiers, who will be Goddamned if they let the jungle eat them up and spit them out." He broke eye contact and stared into the tangle of brush on the riverbank.

"Were you one of those soldiers?" Claire ventured timidly.

His bleak black gaze lasered into hers and for a second, she thought he wouldn't answer. "*Oui.* I have been in the jungle. It was not my friend."

She started to ask when, and where, but he guided the boat along the bank, stopping as gently as a kiss. Unfortunate comparison.

"From here, we walk."

"Walk? Where to?"

"Wherever I say."

Oh, goody. Sharing time was over—as if it had ever started—and now the work would begin.

"NON, NON, NON! Merde! Who taught you to sharpen a knife like that?"

Teaching her how to sharpen blades had been Luc's first task. Claire looked into Luc's sourpuss face from where she knelt over a wicked-looking knife and a whetstone. "The camp counselor." Citronella-scented sweat ran down her face, stinging her eyes even more than regular sweat. At least her salt provided valuable minerals for the cloud of buzzing bugs around her.

Luc made a uniquely French sound of disgust, a cross

between a huff and snort. "Your camp counselor was an idiot. Either that, or you weren't paying attention that day."

She wondered if the knife were sharp enough to stab him in the leg or something else nonvital. "Why don't you show me the right way?" She gave him the best kiss-my-ass smile a Virginia-bred young lady could muster.

Grumbling, he knelt behind her, fresh as a daisy. "Like so." He grasped her hand that held the hilt of her brand-new survival knife, and the one bracing the whetstone. Claire froze as his arms encircled her. How did the man smell so clean and sexy in the middle of a swamp?

He angled her thumb against the blunt edge and slowly helped her draw the blade back toward her in a smooth slicing motion. "Like that. Light pressure, gliding it smoothly. Stroke it across the stone." He flipped over the blade and stone and showed her how to hone the other side.

"That wasn't too bad." Claire fought the urge to fan herself, and not from the sticky heat or bugs.

He let go of her and stepped away. "Now repeat that a dozen times."

"Oh. It's not sharp enough now?"

He sighed. "'A dull knife is a dangerous knife,'" he recited in a singsong voice. "It will slide when you want to cut and it will cut when it stops sliding— probably when it reaches your hand. Now get moving. I have a couple machetes for you to sharpen."

Claire bent over the stone and dutifully sharpened the edges, finally holding it up for his inspection.

He gave a grunt and handed her a big, fat leaf. "Not bad. Cut through this."

It sliced the leaf cleanly. Geez. She hoped she wouldn't cut herself.

"Now the machetes." He pulled them out of a bag, and she recoiled a bit. My goodness, were they big and nasty-looking. He grabbed the hilt of one and slid it from its sheath, looking like a pirate pulling out his cutlass for a bit of pillaging.

And of course, there had to be a whole different way to sharpen machetes since the blade didn't need to be quite as sharp as her knife. After much eye-rolling on his part, he proclaimed her work "adequate, but nothing to be proud of," and she contemplated hitting him in the head with the hilt.

Fortunately, her good breeding prevented violence like that. That, and the fact she had no idea how to get back to his truck. Her stomach rumbled. "What time is it?"

He checked the sun from his cross-legged seated position. "Late morning. Why? You got somewhere you gotta be?"

She gritted her teeth. "No, I was wondering when you usually ate lunch out here. Off the land," she added, parroting his words.

"We eat after we purify water, and make shelter and a fire. Unless you plan to eat sushi or raw rabbit, you need a fire. Or we could go digging for grubs and worms. You don't need to cook those to eat them."

Claire grimaced. Her stomach had definitely stopped rumbling. Talk about eating off the land—more like eating stuff buried *in* the land.

Luc scowled at her. "Don't you make that prissy face at me no more, you. They are pure protein and will keep your body from cannibalizing your muscle tissue. Weak muscles won't get you far." He tossed her a canteen. "Drink. This is the last of the water we brought. We are on our own now."

And wasn't that the truth.

Luc HAD TO GIVE Claire some credit for not whining, but he wasn't about to praise her, not when she was greener than spring grass and rawer than the bluegills flopping around at their feet. She at least had been fishing before, even if she'd admitted her father had always cleaned the fish.

"Time to take that nice sharp knife of yours and let it do its job."

"Right." She stared down at the bluegills and took a deep breath. "Tell me what to do."

He walked her through scaling the first fish, which she managed okay. Several scales flew up and landed in her hair and on her cheeks as she scraped away, catching the midafternoon sun like those sparkles girls put on themselves before going to the bar.

She caught her plump lip between white teeth, turning the fish this way and that to clean the head and tail. He caught shadowy glimpses of her cleavage where she'd unbuttoned a couple buttons in the humid heat, especially when she leaned over to examine what she was doing. Sweat rolled down her neck and disappeared between her breasts.

He shifted uneasily, wanting to chase those droplets with his tongue. Who would have thought watching a woman scale a fish could be so sexy?

"All done!" She held up the glassy-eyed creature proudly—the fish, not Luc, who felt about as dazed. Well, the next step would be enough to cool any man's jets.

"Time to gut it."

Her face fell. "Right." She poked tentatively at the fish belly with her knife.

"No, not like that." Giving into a foolish impulse, he curved his arms around her like he had before with the knife sharpening. It hadn't been a good idea to touch her then and it certainly wasn't a better idea now.

"Okay. So show me." Her voice was a bit husky as he cradled her. She smelled of citronella, sweat and fish, and it aroused him more than the most expensive French perfume.

He'd show her, all right. Would he toss the damn fish away and roll around in the leaves and twigs with her, licking her until she was wet all over and eager for him? Or would he fight his trashy urges and keep his dick in his pants like he'd bragged to Olie he would?

Merde, merde, merde. It sure sucked—and not in a fun way—to keep a promise to his CO. And to Claire. Because if he gave in and screwed her silly like he'd been dying to, he'd never do anything else with her. She'd finish her survival training not knowing anything except how to sharpen a knife, how to scale a fish and how to sexually satisfy one extremely horny Green Beret. Not much help. Although that last part sounded very, very nice....

"Luc?" She licked her lips. "What now?"

He sighed again. "All right, insert the tip of the knife like so...."

THE FISH ACTUALLY DIDN'T taste too bad, smoky from its time over the fire she had built. Claire was glad she'd remembered another thing from her time at camp. Of course Luc had stomped all over her triumph by reminding her that the tinder and kindling was much drier here than in the jungle. Well, pooh to him!

She picked up another chunk of fish from the big green leaf she was using as a plate and popped it into her mouth, too hungry to care that she was the one who had cut its head off and ripped its insides out with her bare hands. That last bit had been a bit gross, but she guessed hunger was a powerful motivator. She never wanted to be hungry enough to eat grubs and other assorted larvae. She wondered if Luc had ever eaten larvae and decided that of course he had. Probably ate them by the handful, like popcorn.

He sat cross-legged about six feet from her, eating silently. When he wasn't ragging on her, he made absolutely no noise. And the swamp, or wetlands or whatever an ecologist might call it, was plenty noisy. Frogs clicked and croaked, birds whistled and honked, and the treetops rustled in the breeze.

Claire looked around. She didn't know if she'd ever been so isolated. Physically, at least. She was used to emotional isolation. Ever since her mother had died, she had been very alone, even among thousands of people in the midst of D.C.

She looked over at Luc, who stared into the fire. He was an enigma to her. Earlier, he'd had a larger-than-life charisma, drawing her attention like a honeybee to a flower. Now, it was as if he had sucked every last bit of his presence inside him and was no more there than the wisps of smoke climbing through the treetops.

Suddenly, she couldn't stand it—she had to get connected to someone, even if he wasn't interested in connecting to her. "Luc!"

He turned slowly to her, his thousand-yard stare sharpening as he focused on her.

She forced a smile. "What next?" He still didn't say anything, and Claire found herself babbling to fill the void. "I figure it's probably late afternoon, so we should probably decide where to pitch our tents before it gets dark, right? I've seen plenty of movies where they try to make camp late at night and it takes forever to pitch the tent and it always collapses anyway. And the mosquitoes—"

"Claire." His quiet tone cut in to her monologue. "You ever just sit and be?"

"Be what?"

He shook his head. "No, I suppose not."

"What does that mean?" She was starting to get angry now. Hadn't she done everything he'd asked today? Sharpened frightening blades, impaled worms on fishing hooks, even eviscerated some poor fish.

"Your mind runs a million miles an hour, Claire. I can practically see the brain waves buzzing off your head."

"Thanks, I guess. So what's the problem?"

"You spend too much time in your head, you're not gon' be a part of anything else." He gestured at the branches and the patches of bright blue sky above them. "You noticing any of this? Or are you trying to figure out what happens next, and what you're gon' have to do, and what I'm gon' do?"

"I don't think I'll have much luck figuring out that last one," she told him tartly.

She startled a quick smile out of him. He shook his head. "Close your eyes, Claire."

"Why?" She gave him a narrow stare. "Are you going to leave me here and sneak off and then I have to spend the night by myself?"

"Trust me, Claire. Close your eyes."

She gave him one last glare and squeezed her eyes shut. If he ditched her in the middle of freaking nowhere, he'd be sorry, although she wasn't sure how she'd do that. Maybe track him down and talk his ears off, since he didn't seem to like that.

"Claire." His deep, French-accented voice cut through her revenge fantasies and inspired some different ones. "Listen to the woods. Listen to the wind, the animals, the water."

Her eyes flew open. "Oh, are we doing guided meditation? I've done this before in hatha yoga class, except we imagined blue balls of light hovering over each chakra—"

He made a strangled sound. "Enough with the blue balls of light! Now close your damn eyes!"

"Fine." She arranged herself cross-legged with her hands in an obvious yoga mudra position before closing her eyes. "Okay, I'm listening. Wow, it's noisy out here."

"Shh. You can't talk and listen at the same time."

Since he wasn't going to let her out of this guided meditation, which it actually was, whether he wanted to admit it or not, she decided to give it a try. Like she had said before, it was a noisy place.

She concentrated on picking out different animal sounds—a small frog's chirp, a big frog's croak, so many different birds she couldn't tell them apart. Then the wind in the trees, swishing and brushing by the leaves.

It shifted and blew some smoke in her face and she fanned it away. Another good reason to keep her eyes closed.

Once the smoke cleared, Claire was surprised at how much she could smell with her eyes closed. She never really considered that sense too much, except when she was picking out body lotions or when she was hungry and everything smelled good.

She recognized Luc's scent right away. A bit of salty sweat, a bit of smoke and a more subtle masculine musk that she'd smelled as he had put his arms around her to instruct her.

What could she do to encourage him to take that further? He seemed impervious to their nearness, or else did a good job hiding it. If the dictionary had an entry for mental toughness, his picture would be next to it.

Maybe she would have to develop her own mental toughness and seduce *him.* She didn't think she'd ever really done that with a man. Sure, she'd smiled and put on sexy dresses, but it was to be expected that the man did the chasing. It was his nature, after all. Especially the nature of a man who chased people for a living.

"Stop thinking, Claire. Try *being.*" His command cut through her planning, and she went back to "being," whatever that meant.

To her surprise, it was easier this time. She found herself swaying in time to her breathing, the ground solid and anchoring her. Luc's presence didn't distract her anymore, although she was aware of him. It really came down to Claire and what she had to learn to take care of herself. For the first time, the training didn't seem scary or impossible. Her mother would be proud of her. Maybe Claire could be proud of herself.

CLAIRE WIPED HER FOREHEAD as she swung her machete at a skinny little tree. Luc was showing her how to build a sleeping platform for a bed, and after he'd described in great detail the slimy, slithering and scaly creatures that roamed the jungle floor at night, Claire had agreed that was a very useful skill. She needed one more sturdy Y-shaped trunk for the fourth corner of the platform and was stripping away small branchlets.

Using the machete actually wasn't so bad, except for the fact she was having trouble keeping her balance and missed some branches. Whew, it was getting hot.

She wiped her forehead again, and this time, Luc noticed. "Hey, when was the last time you took a piss?"

"I beg your pardon." She drew herself up with hauteur worthy of her late Grandmother Cook.

"Excusez-moi, mademoiselle." He gave her a low, mocking bow. *"Quand est la dernière fois que vous avez pissé?"*

It didn't sound any better in French. "Before we left."

"Before we left my friend's house."

Well, technically yes. "Actually, at the hotel."

He swore in French. "Fifteen hours ago? And you didn't think that was a problem?"

She shrugged. "I've been busy." And she hadn't wanted to use the bathroom. Heck, there wasn't any bathroom *to* use.

"Drink." He shoved his canteen at her. The water had a somewhat chemical flavor from the purification tablets, but it was cool and soothing.

"You get a bladder infection or get severely dehydrated and I'll ship you back to your daddy before you can say 'Jack Robinson.'"

He was threatening her? "Shouldn't that be '*Jacques* Robinson?'" She glared at him and drank more water.

He glared back. "Now go into the bushes and do your business."

She looked away. "I don't know how."

She'd finally surprised him. "What?"

"Go outdoors."

He wiped a hand across his face and muttered several words under his breath. "I need to teach you that, too?"

She wanted to dig a hole in the larva-ridden ground and climb in. Mental toughness, mental toughness. She stuck out her chin at him. "Yes, you do."

"It's simple. Pick a tree, pull down your pants and do your business."

"But how do I wipe?"

"You don't."

"Oh, Luc." The idea of having to drip-dry was too much to stand right now.

"Okay." He blew out another French-sounding sigh and selected a leaf from a nearby tree. "Learn this leaf. Memorize it. Love it, because this is your new T.P. *Don't* use *anything* else."

She accepted the leaf and hastily did her business behind some ancient tree. She felt as if she were vandalizing it. Anyway, the next rainstorm would take care of it.

When she returned, he handed her another canteen and pointed her to a big log, where she sat. "Drink."

She tipped it to her mouth and grimaced. "What's that?"

"Treated water with ORS—oral rehydration salts. You'll need to drink all of this plus another. I want to see you running into the woods with another tree leaf within two hours."

"Fine." She forced herself to drink because she knew he'd meant it about sending her home. How humiliating that would be—not even managing twelve hours in the wilderness. Poor Claire, people would snicker, sent home because she couldn't pee in the woods.

She chugged the rest of the canteen and he handed her another. "Here's our next lesson—the jungle is full of fresh water. There's no reason to get dehydrated or overheated. One school of thought says to drink what you can find and get rid of the parasitic infections later.

But that's a last resort. So treat your water." He went on to describe several treatment methods, as well as how to drink from water vines and how to catch rainwater in a variety of containers. "San Lucas gets four hundred inches of rain per year—about ten times what Virginia gets, so that's plenty. You still have to treat it since you don't know what it carried down from the trees, but it's easy."

Claire was beginning to recover, with her second canteenful sloshing around in her stomach, and watching Luc's firm lips shape words and sentences was a lot of fun. His five-o'clock shadow only made him look more dashing and dangerous. Apparently the only danger he ran away from was the notion of having sex with her. She didn't know if that was a compliment or not.

"Claire! Claire!" He scowled at her. "Are you paying attention to me?"

"Of course." She'd been drinking in every detail of his rock-hard body under the black T-shirt and green camo pants. But he meant if she was paying attention to what he was saying. She repeated the last few paragraphs of his lecture, grateful for how she could remember large chunks of information presented orally. Her brain had a digital audio recorder.

"Okay." He slitted his eyes, not quite believing her. "You need to finish your sleeping platform if you're better." He extended his hand to help her stand and she accepted.

He misjudged her weight and pulled a little too hard, dragging her chest-to-chest with him. She stared into his eyes. They weren't quite solid black but had some gold flecks in them. "Luc," she whispered, her breasts nestled against his solid torso.

"Claire," he whispered back. "I need you…."

"What?" Were his defenses crumbling faster than she'd hoped?

"I need you to…get off my foot and get busy!" His last words were almost a shout as he set her away from him. "Gon' go hunt for dinner now. Don't let the fire go out unless you'd prefer snake sushi."

She slumped in disappointment as he disappeared into the brush. Then she remembered his last words. Snake sushi? Her stomach churned. She fed the fire with some dry branches and chanted under her breath, "Tastes like chicken, tastes like chicken." And no chance for dessert tonight—granola bars *or* Luc. Both were off the menu.

THE SNAKE ACTUALLY HAD tasted like chicken, and Luc had showed her some wild plants that were so obviously onions that even she couldn't goof that part up and poison them both. The sun was setting beyond the trees and Claire slapped at several mosquitoes that had come out for blood.

Luc looked up from where he was poking at the fire. "Time to get ready for bed. Don't forget to brush your teeth with the treated water."

Claire nodded. She was beat after only getting a few hours of sleep last night in Luc's truck and working hard in the woods all day. She trudged off to her "pee tree" and gave herself a quick evening toilette. Not quite the spa tub and six-nozzled shower stall that she was used to. Heck, not even the toilet she was used to. Oh, well. There would be none of that at the settlement at Río San Lucas anyway. Pretty soon she would get used to it.

She walked back into the camp and stared at what was going to be her bed. Luc had checked the supports and leafy branches crossing them, and had pronounced the sleeping platform sturdy enough. He had rigged her mosquito netting to a branch above so it dangled over her bed like a princess canopy. To be on the safe side, she squirted on more insect repellent.

"Ready?" He straightened from the log and came to check on her.

"Ready." She hopped awkwardly onto the sleeping platform, trying not to wince as the branches she'd used for bedding poked her in several tender places.

He showed her how to tuck the netting around herself. "Make sure you always, always do this. Mosquitoes can carry four different kinds of malaria, dengue fever and even yellow fever. Malaria medicine and vaccinations are never one hundred percent effective for everybody."

Claire sighed. She was so tired that if a six-foot-long mosquito had swooped down on her like an eagle on a Chihuahua, she wouldn't have batted an eye. "You sure do tell sweet bedtime stories, Luc." She yawned. "Now unless you're going to kiss me good night, you probably should get some rest, too."

He backed away, his expression unreadable in the flickering firelight. "Good night, Claire. We're getting up at oh-dark-thirty tomorrow."

"Great." Claire snuggled into the branches, not even caring that one poked her in the butt. Tonight was no time to be the lead character in "The Princess and the Pea." The branches shifted ominously under her. Or more likely, she'd be the kid in the cradle after the bough broke.

5

LUC HAD HAD THE SAME crappy night's sleep as Claire since he'd woken up every time she shifted position, obviously uncomfortable in her bed of boughs. She had finally drifted off to sleep around 4:00 a.m. as far as he could tell, just when his internal clock was telling him to get up.

He rolled out of his shelter and took care of a few early morning hygiene tasks. After starting the fire again for some coffee, he strolled to Claire's bed and stared down at her. Sleeping Beauty she was not, with several mosquito welts on her neck where her net had gaped and a red scratch on her cheek where a branch had caught her. Her mouth hung open and she was snoring slightly, as if the woods had activated some hay fever.

So why did he have the urge to pull the netting aside and kiss every single injury on her warm ivory skin until they both felt a lot better?

He knew it was a bad idea—Claire Cook was a pretty society girl who got a bee in her bonnet to go out in the big, bad world to do some good. He shook his head. And she couldn't find anything to do back home in Virginia?

Maybe she needed to get away from her father to do anything besides shop and have her cute peach toenails painted. He understood that well enough—he'd left home at eighteen to attend Tulane University, desperate to see something besides the backwoods of Louisiana. He'd messed around with odd jobs the summer after graduating from college and that fall had been the fall of 2001. After seeing the deaths of Americans at the hands of terrorists on live network TV, Luc had shown up at the army recruiting depot September 12.

The Army had taught him more than he could have imagined, and now it was his turn to pass his knowledge on. "Wake up, Claire." He reached through the gap in the netting and shook her shoulder.

"Go 'way," she muttered, slapping at his hand. He stared down at her. Civilians. Well, she was his "army of one," as the old recruiting ads used to say.

"On your *feet!*" he bellowed in his best drill sergeant imitation.

She jerked to a sitting position, her bloodshot eyes staring wildly. "What? What?" She focused on Luc. "Oh, you startled me half to death."

"Rise and shine, we're burning daylight." Without waiting to see if she was awake, he checked his map. "Today we work on map-reading and navigation. You got a good sense of direction?"

"Um. Sure."

Luc raised an eyebrow at her hesitant reply. "I take that as a 'no'."

"I could use some practice," she admitted, swinging her feet out of the shelter. She'd changed into shorts after going to bed and her legs were long, smooth and tanned. He gripped the metal compass case hard, rather than run his hand up her calf.

She started to stand and he stopped her. "Not in bare feet."

"Oh, right. You were telling me last night about all the icky ground parasites that can burrow into your skin." She reached for her boots and a fresh pair of socks that had been sitting in the tops of her boots.

He stopped her again. "Shake out your gear first."

She shook out the socks. "See? Nothing to worry about."

"Fine. Now the boots."

With an indulgent sigh, she dumped over one boot and fastened it onto her foot without incident. The second was another story.

Claire squealed, hopping around on one foot. "What—what the heck is that?"

Luc shook his head. "Brown recluse spider. Along with the black widow, one of two venomous spiders found in the U.S. Distinguished by its dark brown, sometimes yellow color with a black line pointing to the spider's rear. Venom occasionally causes tissue necrosis at the site of the bite."

"Venomous? Tissue necrosis at the site of the bite?"

"Yes, Claire. They crawl into close spaces to hide and bite people when they stick in their hands—or feet." The spider scuttled away toward the leaf litter and Luc stomped on it with his boot.

Wide-eyed, she stared at its mangled remains with disgust.

"Shake out your gear. In the jungle, you'll have spiders way bigger than this, lizards, centipedes, millipedes, ants—you name it." He handed her the boot.

"Yes, Luc." She gave it another vigorous shake and peeked into the inside for good measure before gingerly lacing her foot into it. She grabbed a T.P. leaf from her stash and ducked into the brush.

When she came back, she reached for her tiny bottle of hand sanitizer and squirted it over her hands.

He rolled his eyes. "That crap stinks to high heaven. What are you doing in the woods that you need that junk for?"

She wrinkled her nose at him. "Good bathroom hygiene is important for good health."

"O-kay." Once she got to San Lucas, she'd probably faint to see people washing, babies pooping and animal carcasses being cleaned in the local drinking water.

"Do you have any more purified water? I'm kind of thirsty." And probably hungry, too, judging by the way she looked around hopefully.

"What are our options for potable water?" He wanted to see if she remembered.

"Since we are at low altitude—any lower and we'd be underground—we bring the water to a boil and continue to boil for a minute."

Very good, but he wasn't going to tell her that. Soldiers didn't get trained by touchy-feely stuff. And she wouldn't get trained at all if he kept combining Claire and touchy-feely in the same thought. "And option two?"

"If you have no fire, drop an iodine-based water-purifying tablet in one liter of water, let sit for about a half hour and enjoy the chemical-flavored goodness."

"Better than parasite-flavored goodness. And if the water is particularly nasty, drop in a second tablet and filter out the scum with your teeth."

"Gross, Luc." She made to sit down on a log but he stopped her.

"Grab your groundsheet. Never sit on bare wood or ground."

"Why, more parasites?"

"Exactly." He himself was squatting at the fire's edge. He was used to it, not being around chairs for weeks at a time. He had poured her a cup of coffee and offered it to her when she returned with her ground-sheet.

She looked into the metal mug in surprise. "I thought we were living off the land. Did you pick, roast and grind some coffee beans while I was asleep?"

"No talking back to your commanding officer." He drank his scalding brew with a happy sigh. God, had he missed French roast in Afghanistan.

"Got any non-dairy creamer?" Her lips pursed gently as she blew into the mug. Her soft, pampered hands wrapped around the mug while she moved her mouth into the perfect kissing position before drinking a dainty sip. "Luc? Luc?"

"What? No, no creamer, and no coffee filter, either. We drink our coffee black in Special Forces—puts hair on your chest."

She stared at his chest where he'd tossed on another black T-shirt after a quick wash in the river. "You must have a lot of hair on your chest."

His nipples tightened at her sultry tone.

"Well?" She pursed her lips and blew again, her dark gaze never leaving his.

"I've never had any complaints." He gulped at his coffee. The little minx, was she trying to seduce him again? She might think she wanted a bit of fun before she shipped out, but not at the expense of her safety. He wanted to stand up and get away from her, but his compass wasn't the only thing pointing north. "Drink and let's get going. Breakfast isn't going to jump out of the water and onto the fire." He rubbed his stubbly jaw. "Unless I teach you how to gig frogs. Mmm, mmm, mmm, *les andouilles.*" He made some lip-smacking sounds and her expression turned from sultry to disgusted. "What, a fancy girl like you never ate frogs' legs at one of those fine French restaurants in our nation's capital?"

She shook her head.

"Too bad. Maybe we can find some wild onions or garlic to flavor them."

"Do I really have to eat frogs?" Her voice was almost a whisper.

He raised an eyebrow. "What did I tell you about insects?"

"They're pure protein and keep your body from cannibalizing your muscles." Her mouth pulled down. Whatever her squeamishness, she was definitely no dummy, quoting almost word-for-word what he told her.

"Frogs are the same, except with bones. And you gotta be fast to catch them. You got fast hands, Claire?" He cursed silently as she smiled at his Freudian slip.

"I've never had any complaints."

Word-for-word again. Too bad he couldn't tell her the words he longed to tell her.

CLAIRE STARED AT THE stick holding the fishing line that would hopefully catch their dinner. After two days of fish, she was about to grow gills.

If she weren't so exhausted, she'd be bored out of her skull. Instead, creeping mental numbness dulled her so much, she hardly noticed the blisters popping up on her little toes, the cramps in her calves and the throbbing ache in her lower back. Sitting on the hard ground did that to a person. Not that she was complaining or anything, at least not out loud.

She sighed again and unbuttoned her shirt. The

breeze cooled her bare stomach so well that she took the shirt off altogether. Her gray sports bra covered more than enough compared to the lacy lingerie she preferred but didn't have with her. She could have used another weapon to break down Luc's resolve.

She looked around idly, still self-conscious about sitting in the open wearing only her bra, but she was alone. Luc was off communing with nature, or conquering it and stomping all over it, more likely. He had said something about checking the traps they had set in the morning. She had no idea there were so many ways to lure small animals to their doom. She half hoped none of them would take the bait, but her growling stomach was overcoming more and more of her squeamishness.

Geez, if she was this savage after two days and nights in the wilderness, what would she do after a week? Probably eat raw bugs and cheerfully club alligators and hand-tan their skin. Claire snickered. What every stylish Virginia girl wanted: a purse from the alligator she killed herself.

The fishing line jerked, stirring Claire out of her hunger-induced fashionista fantasy of matching alligator hiking boots. She leaped up from the ground and grabbed the pole. "Easy, easy," she muttered, not wanting to lose this fish. Lifting gently, she pulled a good-size silver fish from the water. "Yay!" She grasped the fish behind the gills and unhooked it, wiping her slimy hand off on her shorts. The poor thing flopped around on the groundsheet. "Sorry, Charlie," she said, parroting the old canned-tuna ad, and laughed.

She reached for another worm and baited the hook. Janey should see her now. A girl who hadn't even done dishes without gloves was manhandling, or woman-handling, invertebrates with ease. Heck, someday she might even eat one! Or not, as something oozed from the worm. She grimaced and threw the line in.

Not much breeze was passing by, but enough to keep the bugs off anyway. Who would have thought the swamp would be somewhat scenic?

"Nice little bluegill you caught."

Claire leaped about four feet into the air. She hadn't heard Luc come up behind her at all. "Geez, Luc, you scared the tar out of me!"

He squatted beside her, his black gaze taking in her bare shoulders and tummy. "I made extra noise to see if you'd notice me. You can't afford to daydream out here."

"Yes, Luc." He was right with that one. "Did *you* catch anything?" She angled her shoulders so her breasts squished together for some cleavage. Obvious, but hey, it was the best she could do with a gray cotton bra.

He gestured at a stick leaning against a big oak tree. Several furry blobs hung from it.

"Oh. Rabbits." She'd eaten those from her dad's hunting trips, but they'd been cleaned and cooked for her. "They look so…sad."

He raised an eyebrow. "They're dead. They're not sad anymore. Not sad like you'd be without any dinner tonight."

Her fishing line jerked again. "Um, do you mind if I stay here and fish?" To underline her request, she pulled out another medium-sized fish and set it next to the other.

He opened his mouth in protest but she touched his arm. He was hot and hard under her touch, little black springy hairs tickling her fingertips. "Please? I know I need to learn how to…what's the phrase for processing animals?"

"Skin and gut?"

She grimaced. "Clean and dress was what I was trying to say. I promise, I'll do it the next time."

He stared into her eyes, his dark gaze unreadable, and then he stared down at her hand on his arm. She jerked it away. "I'm sorry, I'm covered in fish slime again. I really need a bath."

"I expect I'll need one, too, after cleaning all those rabbits by myself."

She smiled at him in relief. "Thank you, Luc."

He shook his head. "I'm not doing you any favors this way. Being squeamish is a good way to be hungry. You can clean those fish by yourself 'cuz you're working your way up to mammals soon." He straightened and walked away.

"Let's trap something that's not cute, okay?"

He stopped, an amazed look on his face. "How's lizard or rat sound?"

She made a sound of distress and he grinned. "Gotcha, *cher*." Silently and with quick steps, he reached the string of rabbits and picked them up. It wasn't until he'd disappeared into the woods that she realized he'd called her *cher* and not Claire.

Cher meant *honey* or *sweetie* and was quite the slip of his normally guarded tongue, she mused as she baited the hook again and tossed it back. Maybe her gray bra was more powerful than she expected.

LUC STARED INTO THE fire that night, mentally begging Claire to get tired and go to bed. By herself. He was finding it harder and harder to resist her. No pun intended. He flicked a glance at her, the flames lighting the curves and planes of her face. She had the most flawless skin and full, plump lips that she was always slicking with some lip balm, puckering and pouting to make sure they were protected.

He dug his fingers into his knees until his knuckles went white. He had rough, hard hands, too rough for her delicate skin and soft body. His self-control around her was like a knife edge that had been honed too fine— sharp enough to cut but liable to snap at the slightest pressure.

She yawned and stretched, her breasts moving up and down under the fabric. At least she'd put her shirt on when the sun went down.

"Ready for bed?" He hoped his voice didn't sound too eager.

She shrugged. "I really wanted to wash before I go to sleep."

He grunted, immediately disturbed by the images that conjured. "Why bother? You'll need fresh bug spray after you finish."

"I know, but it's been so hot and sticky." She rubbed the nape of her neck. "I think I'm getting prickly heat."

Luc was, too, but not the rash kind.

"You want to check?" She lifted her ponytail of thick, dark hair and bared her nape to him.

"No, no," he said, backpedaling. "You'll need some water to wash with." He brought out the larger container of purified water. "You'll want some privacy, so I'll leave."

"You mean, wash right here?" She looked around nervously.

"Claire, we're in the middle of nowhere. The only other person for miles is me." He figured she was probably imagining local backwoodsmen spying on her through the foliage. "The fire is dying down to limit visibility and I'll reconnoiter the perimeter."

Her face cleared. "If that means keeping an eye out for any Peeping Toms, that sounds good." She went to her duffel bag and collected clean clothes, a washcloth and small bottle of biodegradable soap.

Luc faded away and slipped through the trees. The insects and birds were as noisy as before, not startled by any other human presence. He sniffed the air for any other scent of bug spray or fire. As he expected, nobody was around. Still, he circled their camp slowly and stealthily to keep in practice. He hadn't trained in swampy woodlands for a long time, being stationed in either the urban Middle East or its rocky, mountainous outposts.

His senses heightened as he went, his night vision sharpening as he smelled individual plants and picked out insect and birdsong. The vibrating rumbles of faraway gators bellowing made him smile. Just like home. His anger about being forced away from home on his leave had subsided, but something even more dangerous had replaced it: pure lust.

Why couldn't the congressman's daughter be married, or snooty or less attractive? Instead, Claire was single, available, sweet-natured and sexy enough to make him forget his name.

A hideous noise startled the normal sound-makers into frightened silence. Luc pulled his knife and ran toward the camp, his only thought to get to Claire. He cleared fallen logs and lurking branches with ease and made it to the darkened clearing within seconds. He dropped into a crouch at the edge to assess the situation.

Claire was standing alone, illuminated by the bluish light of the full moon. He relaxed briefly and sheathed his knife when he realized the noise was her off-key singing, but then she turned around and he saw everything he'd wanted and everything he shouldn't.

Her hair was piled on her head as she leisurely soaped the nape of her neck, running the washcloth over her shoulders and arms. Sudsy water trickled around her plump, round breasts and down to her dark nipples. He held his breath as one soapy blob clung to the peak of her breast before plummeting to the ground below.

"Au clair de la lune," he murmured to himself. "By the Light of the Moon" was an ancient French folk-song, and *Claire* meant *light* or *bright.*

Her skin gleamed silver in the moonlight as if it held light of its own. Her belly curved into full, rounded hips guarding the dark treasure between them. He could only look at her as if she were Diana, the moon goddess come down to the woods to tempt him.

He muffled a groan as she washed her stomach and back, finally reaching between her legs. His own groin throbbed painfully in response. Without thinking, he eased open the first couple of buttons on his camo pants. He was stroking his cock when he realized what he was doing—becoming the Peeping Tom he'd promised to protect her against.

He groaned, cupping himself for a second before buttoning up with some difficulty. He'd promised Olie his word as a Green Beret that he could be trusted around Claire. Hell, he'd promised Claire she could trust him. Watching on her while he crouched in the woods playing with himself was *not* trustworthy, to say the least.

He gave her one last, longing glance and reluctantly turned his back. She continued her out-of-tune serenade as he sat in the darkness, wondering how the hell he would hold out against her charms.

6

CLAIRE FIGURED LUC wasn't interested in her anymore, despite the flash of heat they'd generated in her hotel room. Despite wearing her sports bra as a top all day, Luc wasn't biting at the bait, either avoiding looking at her or else keeping his gaze from her neck upward. She swiped her hand over her face, glad for the light clothing as she finished gutting yet another fish. It had become less revolting, if not less messy.

"Claire?" Luc had come up behind her again, but at least this time she'd heard him.

"All done with the fish. We can eat them for a late lunch if you want." She rinsed off her hands and wiped them dry on her poor abused pants. They practically stood on their own by now.

"In a few minutes. Right now I want to show you a survival kit I always carry." He sat cross-legged on her groundsheet and pulled out a small round tin about the size of a hockey puck. "You need to make one, too, and always, always carry it on your body. In a buttoned pocket, not a purse or backpack."

"I guess I could always stick it in my bra if I need to."

His gaze fell to her breasts before looking away. "Whatever you need to do." He undid the sticky tape around the circumference. "The tape keeps the container waterproof."

"In case I fall out of a boat or something?"

He froze midgesture and slowly opened the can the rest of the way. "Yes. Boating down the main river in Río San Lucas can be dangerous." He pulled out more things than she thought would fit in the tiny container, including waterproof matches and cotton balls soaked in petroleum jelly. She wouldn't have thought of other items, like fishing line and hooks, needles and thread, and even a flexible saw that coiled like a thick jagged wire.

"What is that at the bottom?" She spied a square plastic packet among the wound bandages and antibiotic and painkiller pill tubes.

"Water storage device." He made to repack the tin but she stopped him.

"It's so tiny, how can it hold water?"

He sighed and pulled it out.

"Wait, that's not a water storage device, that's a condom." She wrinkled her nose at him. "Honestly, Luc, I would think under the dire circumstances when you'd need this kit that a condom would be low on the priority list."

Darned if he wasn't blushing a bit under his sun-darkened skin. "Claire, we use prophylactic devices for plenty of things beside their original intent. We cover the rifle barrels with them to keep water from rusting them and we do use them for water storage. They store about a quart of water."

"Really? I had no idea they stretched so far." Claire grabbed the condom out of his hand. "Extra large, ribbed. Is it easier to grip the ribbed ones with wet hands?"

Ha ha, she was making him blush like a tomato. "It was the only kind they had."

"Is that the brand you usually use? I mean for carrying water and covering the tip of your…rifle?"

"Never mind," he growled, stuffing the packet into the tin and repacking the other items. "I figured you wouldn't take this seriously."

She frowned back at him. "Hey, no fair. Haven't I done everything you asked? Haven't I done everything you wanted?"

Luc clenched his fists. "Everything I asked, *oui*. Everything I wanted, *non*." He dragged her into his arms and kissed her. Claire barely had enough time to give a mental cheer before being swamped by the anger, frustration and lust that rolled off him in a passionate wave.

She eagerly opened her mouth under his, his tongue immediately rubbing along hers. He nibbled on her lips as if they were the sweetest candy, biting and sucking on her as if he were starving.

Claire was starving, too, starving for the body she'd been watching surreptitiously for days. She shoved her hands under his T-shirt and moaned at his slick, hot skin. Under her caresses, he was pure muscle and bone with not an ounce of fat. She suddenly felt self-conscious about her not-so-hard body and stopped touching him.

Luc made a sound of protest and pulled her even closer, crushing her breasts against him. She took this as the go-ahead she needed and indulged herself, tracing the indentations of his ribs, the heavy muscle of his back. Her fingers found a thick ridge of skin that marred his smooth perfection.

She pulled away. "What's that?"

"That feels very good."

She pressed into the scar. "That."

"Oh. Shrapnel."

"Shrapnel?" She was about to ask him for details when he pressed kisses from her jaw down to her neck, licking and sucking at her earlobe. His hot mouth sent sensual jolts down to her nipples and even farther south. She moaned his name and wiggled against him.

He broke their kiss. "*Non,* Claire, I shouldn't be doing this. I swore I'd be a gentleman around you, swore I'd keep my hands off you."

So that was why he'd been so standoffish. "I'm releasing you from your promise." She dragged his head down to hers and sucked hard on his bottom lip. He inhaled sharply but pulled away again.

"It doesn't work that way, Claire. A man's word is his honor."

Time for drastic measures. "I know you're an honorable man and you would never do anything to hurt me. That's why I choose you for this." She reached behind her and unsnapped her bra, dropping it on the ground. "I want you, Luc. Life is difficult. There is no dishonor in taking a bit of pleasure where we can."

He swallowed hard at the sight of her bare breasts. "I'm so hard I could hammer in tent pegs. I can't be leisurely or gentle, whispering sweet nothings in your ear."

Her nipples tightened, sending jolts down between her legs. "Will you make me feel good?" She couldn't believe she was seducing a sexy man like Luc in the middle of the day, outdoors, but she'd never wanted anything more.

"Better than you've ever felt before." He wasn't bragging, merely stating a fact.

"Then *oui,*" she whispered, eliciting a wolfish grin from him.

"I like hearing that word on your lips. You gon' say it a lot more times before I'm done with you." Luc stripped off his shirt, revealing what she'd only touched before. His chest was lightly covered in black hair, his coppery nipples pulled into tight disks. Several paler scars marred his skin. "Take off your pants."

She hurriedly unlaced her boots and shoved the rest of her clothing off. An unexpected rush of shyness came over her, and she hunched, curling her arms around her bent knees. He frowned in concern, and she realized he was having second thoughts.

Before he changed his mind, she forced herself to lean on her elbows, the breeze cool on her totally bare-naked body. Outdoors, in the middle of the day, no less.

His eyes darkened with lust, and he quickly made himself as naked as she was. Oh, my. His erection was as powerful as the rest of his body. The sunlight high-lighted its thick head and corded veins running its impressive length. Claire stared at him with a little bit of apprehension and a whole lot of awe.

"*Bébé,* don't keep lookin' at me like that." He acknowledged her gaze by growing even further, a silver drop appearing on his tip.

"Like what?" She rubbed her thighs together to try to ease her matching lust.

"Like you're the sexiest thing ever and you can't wait for me to fuck you."

Heat crept up her face. "I do want you to…" She just couldn't say it. "Do that."

"*Bon.*" He dropped to his knees beside her and cupped her cheek briefly, tracing his hand down her neck, over one breast and the curve of her hip. She dropped her knees apart and he immediately found her hidden nub.

She cried out and tipped her head back. He pushed her shoulder until she rested on the groundsheet. He stared eagerly down at her. "*Très, très belle, toi.*"

She blushed at being called beautiful. Then he stroked her and she forgot all about being embarrassed. His hands were rough but gentle as they brushed her skin. He circled one nipple and the other as they peaked and grew.

His expression was rapt. "Let me taste you, sweet Claire."

He lowered his mouth to one breast, delicately flicking it with his tongue. His fingers made similar motions on her—her…clitoris. If she was brave enough to do this, she could call her body parts what they were. She wrapped her arms around his neck, running her fingers through his thick black hair.

"*Oui,* that is good." He sucked hard on her breast and slipped a finger inside her, making her cry out. His erection jerked where it rested against her hip. "Claire, Claire, I need you so bad." He inserted a second finger, spreading them apart to stroke deep inside her. She cried out again. "You're so hot, *cher,* wet and ready. I know you can take me now."

"Yes, now, now." She couldn't believe this amount of foreplay had aroused her to such a fever pitch.

He took the condom from his kit and quickly covered himself. Kneeling between her legs, he stared down at her, pure lust and concern battling on his face.

She reached up to him. "Come to me, Luc."

He surrendered with a groan and stretched out on top of her. His erection prodded at her, the tip finally going in. She tensed for a second and relaxed as she realized it didn't hurt. He sensed that and quickly entered to the hilt. She gasped and he stopped. "Did I hurt you?"

She quickly shook her head. Filled her and stretched her more than she'd ever been, yes. Hurt, no. She experimentally tightened around him and he jerked inside her.

Sweat beaded on his lip. "Can't hold still, *bébé*, gotta move." He glided in and out of her. "You are paradise. Wrap your long legs around me."

She did, locking her ankles in the small of his back. He groaned again and took her on a wild ride as he pistoned in and out. All Claire could do was clutch his shoulders and hold on. He felt wonderful inside her, and maybe he'd touch her more once he was done.

But to her surprise, the delicious friction of his hard member was more than wonderful. He was rubbing all the right spots, her hips moving to match his. He noticed the difference and grinned down at her. "You're a real hot one, *cher.*" He dropped to his elbows and bit her earlobe. "I bet you can come with just my thrusting."

She protested how impossible that was but he sucked hard on her neck. She clutched his shoulders. "Oh, Luc." Darned if her passage didn't tighten around him even more, and they both groaned.

"Can't last much longer, *bébé. Baise-moi, baise-moi.*"

His raw French excited her. She shook as her

tension built, her head whipping back and forth. He grunted and jolted into her, pushing her halfway off the groundsheet.

Soft cries came from her throat as her heels dug into his rock-hard behind. She arched her back to take all of him as deep as he could go. Their bodies slapped wetly together, their skin sticking and releasing with every motion. She was bound more deeply to him than she'd ever been to a man.

Not wanting to miss a single second, she opened her eyes and stared at him. His face was twisted in agony. He met her gaze. "Come with me, Claire. Right now, with my cock inside you. Jus' think of all the sex juice I got saved for you." He angled himself so he bumped her clitoris over and over.

She gave a brief scream as he swelled inside her even more.

"That's it—scream for me. Now I know how good your pussy feels around me, I'm not gon' let you go." He moved frantically. "Come, dammit, now. Now!"

She wrapped her arms around his shoulders and squeezed down hard on his cock. Amazingly, tremors blossomed, spreading to her sensitive nub and up her belly to her breasts, neck and face. She shook around him as he blasted her self-control to shreds. Her moans crescendoed into a scream.

Luc gave a shout of pure triumph and exploded inside her. He rocked into her supersensitized clitoris, causing a second matching explosion. His mouth fell open as he pounded into her for what felt like an eternity, his face contorted into mindless pleasure. She could only hold on through his marathon climax, marveling at his pent-up desire.

He finally came back to earth. "Ah…" He rested his forehead against her, his black hair soaked with sweat. "That was…that was…"

"Intense?" she suggested.

"Nuclear." He gasped for air and slid partway from her. "Ah, I want to stay here all day."

"Then do." Claire had the delicious feeling she had only seen the tip of the iceberg when it came to Luc's sexual prowess. "I want you to show me everything I've been missing."

He eased from her, his erection still impressive despite his release. They were lucky he hadn't broken the "water storage device." He disposed of it into the fire. "What have you been missing, honey?"

"Sex." The word was strange on her tongue but liberating. "I want more sex and lots of it. I never did it like this before."

"What, outdoors?" He looked puzzled.

"No." She blushed but continued on. "Never, um, climaxed with a man before."

"What?" His shocked expression would have been comical if she hadn't been serious.

She rolled on her side to face him. "It's true. I never met anyone who made me feel like this and I want you to teach me everything you know."

"Everything?" He ran his tongue over his lips. "I lost my virginity when I was fifteen and haven't looked back. I've done things you've never heard of. Things that would scare a sheltered lady like you."

"If you don't show me, I'll go back to Virginia and find someone who will." She was bluffing, but he didn't need to know that.

His eyes narrowed. "You don't mean that."

"I do, Luc. I've been living a protected life, and I mean to change that in the most intimate way possible. I want you to be my teacher."

"Claire, you make it so hard for a man to say no. A gorgeous, naked woman begs me for sex lessons, what do I say?"

"Part of you says yes." She ran her hand down his chest and took his cock in her hand, still slippery from his climax. "What does the rest of you say?"

He closed his eyes as she traced his length. "*Oui.* I can't help myself around you."

She grinned in triumph. He leaped to life under her touch. Several days in the woods, just the two of them as he taught her all sorts of amazing sexual experiences. "Do you have more condoms?"

He nodded. "A whole box. But you're not gonna need one now."

"Why not?"

"You want me to teach you everything?" He folded his hand around hers and moved them up and down his shaft.

"Yes, everything." Claire's breath came faster.

"Then you need to know how to touch me with your hand. Take my edge off." Their hands moved faster. "Make sure I can fuck you for hours after."

She gave a gasp and he grinned. "Why, Mademoiselle Claire, I noticed before but didn't want to embarrass you—it seems that you like dirty talk."

"I…I…"

"Don't worry your sweet li'l self about it." He rolled onto his back, never letting go of her hand. "I won't tell anyone as long as you please me."

"How do I do that?"

"Like this." He dragged her hand to his tip and down to the base in a slow, thorough pattern. Once she had that down, he had her kneel next to him. "Lean over my face."

"What?"

He pillowed his head on his arms. "I want to suck on you. First your sweet titties, and then…" He gave a very male shrug. "Wherever else I want."

A thrill coursed through her. "Yes, Luc." She angled her body so her nipples brushed his stubbled cheeks. She knew it felt good and leisurely rubbed his face back and forth before he pulled one tip hard into his mouth.

She bit back a moan. He hadn't played with her breasts much during their fast and hard coupling. It was difficult to keep a steady pace with her hand.

"I see I'm gon' have to take the edge off you, too."

She shook again as he unerringly found her clitoris. With hard, deft strokes, he had her climaxing and collapsing on top of him. She barely had time to catch her breath before he urged her upright again. "You shouldn't have come before I did. Touch me the right way."

Claire tried to do it the way he wanted, but he kept pinching and sucking her nipples, making her arch and cry his name. He stopped tormenting her with his mouth. "You need to come again, don't you?" He found where her juices had run down her inner thigh and rubbed them into her tender skin.

"Yes, Luc."

"Say, 'yes, please.'"

"Yes, please, Luc."

"What?"

"I need to come again," she whispered. He was spread out on his back like some Middle Eastern pasha, all muscle and slick bronzed skin. Her hand was pale and fragile-looking against his thick, blood-engorged erection. She couldn't believe how he had ensnared her so quickly into such raw sensuality. Cool, quiet Claire, kneeling naked in the woods, begging for a third climax.

"I didn't hear you."

She took a deep breath. "I need to come again."

He gave her a cat-that-swallowed-the-canary smile of triumph. "Damn right you do. You're the hottest piece of ass I've ever seen." His crude words heated her even further. "Spread your legs and ride my fingers."

He slipped two fingers inside her and added a third. She raised and lowered herself on the makeshift shaft and screamed as his thumb pressed her hidden nub. She was wetter than she'd ever been before and he took advantage of it, sliding and spreading his thick fingers. "*Oui,* there." He pressed inside her and she gushed over his hand, crying his name, crying for release that mercifully broke over her.

She collapsed on him, his one hand still buried inside her. With her cheek resting on his damp chest, she saw him reach around her and cup his cock. Half a dozen quick strokes and he finished what she'd started, his seed arcing high into the air as his heart pounded under her ear. She stared at the raw power of his second orgasm coming only minutes after the first.

She stretched out next to him as they both gasped for air. "You do have a lot stored up, don't you?"

"I wasn't lying when I told you I hadn't had sex in a long time. I was able to keep going without it until you broke the dam, *cher.* Now I don't know how I'm gon' get you trained in survival when all I want to do is train you in sex."

"Sex won't interfere, I promise." She crossed her heart, tracing her finger over her bare breast.

He raised an eyebrow. "Oh, yeah? How will we go on hikes when all I want is to pull down your pants and take you against a tree? How will I sit on that log and explain important things to you when all I want is you to kneel between my legs and suck on my cock?"

Claire shivered. "I've never done that to a man before," she confessed.

His grip tightened on her. "You keep telling me things like that, you gon' make me hard again," he rasped.

Claire smiled. She'd never been complimented like that.

"But, Claire, I need to confess something, too."

"What is it?" Had he changed his mind already?

He looked guilty for the first time since they'd met. "I have a tent and sleeping bags in the boat."

"You what?" Her nervousness vanished. "I've been sleeping on a bed of branches with sticks poking me in the butt with nothing but a foil blanket and mosquito netting for cover and you had a tent and sleeping bags?" She twisted her fingers into his chest hair and tugged hard.

"Ow!" He grabbed her hand.

She leaned over him. "What's the matter? The big, tough, Green Beret never had anyone pull on his chest hair before? Better not let the enemy know that or you and your men might wind up as bare-chested as an underwear model."

"At ease, *mam'zelle*." He cupped her neck and pulled her down for a kiss. "You needed to learn to make a bed platform and sleep on it. But if you don't want me to pitch the tent, we could always try doin' it on your platform. Sure hope you built it well...."

She giggled and kissed him again. "Not that well, Luc. Even a sleeping bag on the ground would be a welcome change."

"Don't worry, *bébé*. You and I won't be doing a whole lotta sleepin'."

7

CLAIRE PLODDED THROUGH the woods after Luc. He had decided to find a new spot for their campsite and pitch the tent. The terrain was slightly different, more wooded than swampy and even more secluded. She had enjoyed the boat ride more the second time, but now they were making up for it on foot. It gave her plenty of time to think and plenty of time for second thoughts. How much did she actually know about this man? She had never in her life been so sexually impulsive and was starting to regret it.

Maybe if she got to know him better, it would ease her doubts. She took a deep breath. "So, where are you from, Luc?"

He replied after a pause. "Louisiana."

She wasn't an idiot—he was a Cajun, after all. "Yes, I know that, but which part? North, south, east—"

"South central Louisiana. Near the Atchafalaya Basin."

"What's it like?"

"Hot, muggy."

"Oh, like this?" Claire looked around.

"Some."

She pressed her lips together. "There's this interesting concept you may have heard of. It may not be part of Green Beret training, but it's called 'conversation.' I say something, and you say more than two words back to me."

"How about three?"

She shot daggers at his broad shoulders. He didn't want to talk? She'd fully compensate for it. "My full name is Claire Adeline Cook. My middle name is after my maternal grandmother, who was German, so no jokes about it. I'm an only child but I have a few cousins on my dad's side. I grew up in Virginia and I majored in humanities with concentrations in English and French literature." She thought for a second. "My favorite colors are peach and warm coral, which is actually an orangey kind of red, but that looks better in winter, whereas peach is a pastel better suited for summer. I have a horse named Pumpkin at home, and I won some riding competitions when I was a kid." She paused to drink from her canteen.

He still didn't reply, so she continued doggedly. "My best friend is Janey, whom you met. She's very busy with her army career, so I don't see her often. I enjoy yoga, French cooking and tutoring kids in an after-school reading program." She wound down, suddenly tired of trying to get a response from him.

They walked in silence for a few minutes.

"My full name is Luc Edouard Boudreaux. My middle name is after my father."

Claire stared at his back in amazement. It was the most he'd said about himself, ever. But he continued, "I have six older sisters."

Her eyes bugged out, but she didn't dare say anything to interrupt the flow.

"I have about thirty cousins last I counted, and I majored in English and drama at Tulane. My favorite color is army green, and I had a pet alligator when I was a kid. My best friend is Olie, who's also very busy with his army career, but I see a lot of him."

Claire smiled at his wry sense of humor.

"What else did I miss?"

"Hobbies."

"Running and weightlifting." He fell silent.

"Six sisters?"

"Yeah, I blame them for getting me into the drama thing. They were always dressing me up as the male lead in their plays."

"So that's how you know about Shakespeare."

"I was in a couple productions."

She quoted a few lines from Romeo and Juliet in a girlish English accent.

He slid effortlessly into a flawless accent and quoted the next lines right back to her.

"Very good." She applauded and he turned around to give her a sweeping bow, his machete dipping like an old-fashioned rapier.

"Better now?"

"What?"

He grinned at her. "Now that you know something about me."

Busted. "Yes, I do feel better. You may not believe this, but I don't normally jump into bed with strangers."

"We haven't made it to a bed, yet, *béb*."

That must be short for *baby* in Cajun, kind of like being called "babe." Her face heated. "That's not what I meant."

"I promise not to think less of you, Claire. I'm honored you would break your own rules to be with me."

He had broken his rules, as well, but Claire worried he'd get all noble and self-sacrificing and refuse to come near her again if she mentioned it. She gestured at the wilderness around them. "Out here, rules were meant to be broken, right?"

"You're only allowed to break the ones that don't get you hurt."

She wanted to ask if he meant emotionally hurt, as well, but figured that topic was best left for another time, or perhaps left alone altogether. "So, six sisters— I can't even imagine! What are their names?"

He set off along the trail again. "Let's see— Evangeline is the oldest, then Jolie, Nicolette, Gabrielle, Acadia and finally Adeline right before me."

He said his sister's name with a French accent, but she recognized it. "That's my middle name!"

"So, you see why I wouldn't make fun of your name. Don't want two angry women comin' after me."

"Oh, I think you can handle yourself."

"Claire, you never met Adeline."

CLAIRE WAS STILL SMILING as she helped Luc pitch a tent barely enough for the two of them. That was okay. Like he'd said earlier, who was planning to sleep? She walked to where they'd set their packs. Her feet were sore and her socks soaked.

She pulled out a fresh pair and sat on yet another log to pull off her boots. "Oh, my gosh." Her sock was splotched in blood.

Luc whipped around from where he was checking their coordinates on his map. "What the hell?" He was at her side before she could blink. "Did you step on something, you?"

She peeled off her sock gingerly. The reddened areas she had so carefully cushioned in the morning were raw and bleeding blisters.

"Ah, boo, your poor feet." He tsked like an old lady as he knelt and examined her other foot, which was just as bad. He returned with some water and his first-aid kit before gently lifting one foot to rest on his thigh.

"Boo?" She tried not to wince as he doused her wounds with water before carefully disinfecting and bandaging them.

"What?" He didn't look up, intent on his task.

"What does 'boo' mean?"

He met her glance sheepishly. "It's an old Cajun term of endearment—like 'dear' or 'honey.'"

She smiled despite the pain. So he'd called her the equivalent of "honey" and had answered to it when she'd asked about it. "How on earth did they ever come up with 'boo'?"

"No idea. Cajun French is full of Spanish, African and Indian words. The university linguists adore comin' round with their digital recorders to talk to the *papères* and *mamères*—grandpas and grandmas. My own *mamère* is interviewed every Christmas, Easter and summer break."

"You're exaggerating."

"Not much. She informed us the last academic told her she was a national cultural treasure, so we'd better behave ourselves or she'd pass us a slap." He grinned. "A slap from a national cultural treasure still stings pretty good."

So did her feet. "I don't think I'll be able to hike very much tomorrow. Is there something we can work on close to camp?"

He frowned and finished doctoring her. "You think I make you hike on those feet, you?" She knew he was getting irritated when he added French-style reflexive pronouns. "What kind of man do you think I am?"

"A good one." She leaned forward and kissed his forehead.

He looked up, startled. "I don't know 'bout that, Claire."

"Well, I do."

He grunted and packed away his supplies before

pulling out her canvas sneakers she wore in camp at night to let her boots dry.

"I don't think my feet will fit in those anymore."

"Sure they will." He pulled out his razor-sharp knife and made several slits in the shoes to allow for her bandages. When he was done they looked more like sandals.

She eased her feet into them. "Thanks for taking such good care of me, Luc."

"*De rien,* it was nothin'." He shook his head. "Just because I broke my word about certain things doesn't mean I won't look after you." He picked up the water purifier and busied himself refilling the canteen.

He was still feeling guilty for giving in to her sexually. She smiled. "Luc?"

"Yes?"

She stood, wobbling slightly in her jerry-rigged shoes. He was at her side immediately. "Can you help me to the tent? I want to get off my feet."

He swept her into his arms and carried her to the tent flap, setting her gently down on the sleeping bags. After three nights of tree branches, they were heavenly soft.

"Better?" He knelt next to her.

She stroked his knee, daring to glide her hand up his thigh when he offered her no resistance. "I could be a lot better if you helped distract me."

His black eyes glittered in the dim light. "What kind of distraction did you have in mind, boo?"

"This." She moved her hand a few inches over and found his growing erection.

"You want this?" He undid his gear belt and unbuttoned his fly. She freed him from his briefs, cradling him with trembling hands as he swelled under her touch. "You want all of it?" He grabbed her wrist and made her cup his heavy sac. His weight and power sent a wet gush between her legs.

She nodded.

"Then lick me."

To call her unskilled in that area was an understatement. Still, she bent her head and licked him as if he were a big purple ice cream cone.

He jerked under her tongue, leaving an unfamiliar taste of salt and musk. *"C'est bon, ça."*

Good, that meant he liked it. She licked a few more times but he cradled the back of her head and urged her deeper. She struggled a bit, and he looked at her in alarm.

She paused and took a deep breath, then tentatively opened her mouth wider. He stopped her.

"I'm sorry if I wasn't any good at that." She blinked hard. So much for being a wild woman.

"I didn't stop you 'cause it made me feel bad—I stopped you because it didn't make *you* feel good." He nuzzled her neck until she tipped back her head. "I only want to make you feel good." He pressed kisses down her neck to her collarbone and rapidly undressed her, being extra careful of her feet. When he was done, she lay naked on the sleeping bags. "Claire, don't you look pretty enough to eat."

"Eat?" Did that mean what she thought?

"You ever had a man eat you up before?" He pressed his fingers between her thighs. "Take you into his mouth right here?"

She shook her head, wincing. She'd been in the woods for days without a proper shower, for goodness' sake. How could he want to do…that?

"Okay, *cher.*" His tone was gentle. "Someday soon, though. You'll love it, I promise."

Yeah, right. But her embarrassment was quickly forgotten as he stroked her clitoris. "The tongue, it's not so different from the finger. Hot, wet and slick, it slides over this little jewel back and forth, back and forth."

Her hips rotated as his hypnotic voice filled the tent.

"Your body, it tells me what you like. The finger, it touch, but the tongue, oh, the tongue, it taste what you like." He withdrew his hand and licked his fingers.

Her eyes flew wide with shock. "Luc!"

"Mmm, you taste go-ood." He grinned down at her with no signs of disgust. "Can't hardly wait to get my face snuggled up there." He put his fingers back. "Now if I was eatin' you up, I'd use both hands to spread your legs wide like so. And I'd take my thumbs to pull back the hood from your little jewel, like so. Then I real gentle tease you, an' tease you with flicks of my tongue—like this." As he played with her innermost flesh, Claire swelled and grew under his slow, instructive touch. How did he know the secrets of her body when she'd never discovered them for herself?

"Well, would you look at that? My fingers are telling me you like showing me your sweetness. Your little *chatte* is getting all pink and plump."

"*Chatte?*"

He gave her a sly smile. "*Chatte* is a female cat."

Cat, kitten—oh. "I never learned that slang word in French class."

"I should hope not." He gave her a look of mock outrage. "If all you fancy prep school girls went around petting your *chattes,* you never get any homework done."

She blushed. "I never did."

"Did your homework? You naughty girl."

"Not that! The other."

"No time like the present." He caught her hand and brought it down to her, um, well, *chatte.* She tried to pull away but he wouldn't let her. "I told you I would teach you everything you needed to know. You need to know this."

He moved her fingers across her clitoris. "Learn what you like. Fast and hard?"

She choked back a moan as he strummed her like she was a guitar.

"Or slower, in circles?"

"I…like it…all," she gasped.

"*Bon.* Now you gon' play with yourself while I fuck you."

She stared at him. "Aren't you, um, going to take off your clothes?"

"No, don't think so." He bent down to kiss her nipple. "I think you might like my soft T-shirt rubbing your titties." He pressed his chest against her bare breasts and she groaned. It did feel good.

"And I think you'd like my rough pants slapping your sweet li'l ass." He stroked himself a few times, his big hand working up and down his erection. "That's real good. Maybe I touch myself, then you touch yourself, we see who comes first?"

"No, Luc, I can't wait." The sight of him pleasuring himself was extremely arousing. He stared raptly at her naked breasts, hard nipples and wide-open thighs as if she were his most secret fantasy.

And he was hers. She took a deep breath and touched her clitoris. He groaned, and she took that for encouragement, stroking herself with more boldness than she ever had. She really did swell under her fingers, her juices easily slicking the way. Juicy enough for Luc to slide right in and mix his with hers. She wanted his bare skin inside her, his clothing rubbing her. "Come inside me," she whispered. The pressure was driving her crazy.

"Where, *cher?*"

"My *chatte*. Please," she added.

He stroked himself a few more times. "Since you asked so nice…" He sheathed himself in a condom and moved between her thighs. "Take me, *béb.*"

This time, he slid right in, locking them together.

"Ah, Claire, so fuckin' tight and hot. I never want to leave you." He kissed her, his tongue deep in her mouth. She sucked on it hard like she'd wanted to suck on his other body part and he groaned.

Claire instinctively raised her hips as he slid in and out of her. He broke their kiss to gasp for air. "Ride me, Claire. You ever get turned on bouncing up and down on that saddle of yours?"

She nodded. Not that she'd known what it meant at the time. Before she could say anything, he'd scooped her up and rolled onto his back so she was sitting on his cock, totally naked and exposed, her hair a mess and her breasts bouncing all over. "Ride me hard, Claire. I want to see your *chatte* coming up and down my cock, your ass rubbing my balls. Do it."

Claire hesitated for a second but he wrapped his big hands around her hips and lifted her up and down for a few seconds until she got the rhythm. After that, her body knew what to do.

She rose and fell on him, her hands braced on his taut chest. He tipped his head back and matched her rhythm. She decided for a little variety and swiveled her hips, leaning forward and back. She swore his eyes crossed as he swelled inside her even more.

Luc let go of her hips and squeezed her breasts, her nipples rubbing his rough palms. He found her rock-hard nipples and pinched them both at the same time. She cried out as the sensation shot straight down to her clitoris.

"Touch yourself again," he groaned. "Can't last much longer with you riding me like a stallion."

She slipped her finger over her clitoris, her nail brushing the base of his shaft. They groaned in unison. "Oh, Luc." She was shaking almost too hard to keep moving, but the pressure inside her was so delicious she never wanted it to end.

"Hurry, hurry," he urged her. His hands mapped her breasts, belly, bottom, blurring the boundaries between his body and hers. She contracted around him and he looked at her with glassy eyes. "Now?"

"Now!"

His fierce thrusts made her melt all over him, her *chatte* throbbing as he pounded deep inside her. She moaned his name, begged and pleaded with him, but he was merciless, dragging her into a second orgasm before letting go himself.

"Claire, oh, Claire…" He broke off into a shout of sexual triumph, bucking and pulsing as he emptied himself in a long, powerful climax.

THIGHS TREMBLING, SHE collapsed onto his cotton-clad chest. "Oh, Luc, that was wonderful." She tried to catch her breath as he rubbed her bare back.

"Wonderful," Luc echoed in a daze, floored by how wild she had been after her first tentative attempts. If he wasn't mistaken, that was the only time she'd ridden a man to completion. He helped her ease off him and tucked her into his side.

She rested her head on his shoulder as he stroked her silky hair. "Tell me, how does such a sexy woman make it to your age without certain experiences?"

"I assume you mean sexually?"

He nodded. "Not that I'm complaining. It gives me great pleasure to be your teacher." That was an understatement. One of his romance-reading previous girlfriends had called him an "alpha male," kind of like the alpha wolf that dominated the pack and earned his pick of the females.

And Claire was the best he'd ever picked. But he still wasn't sure why'd she'd picked him.

"It's kind of a boring story."

"We have all night." He kissed the top of her head.

"Well, I was almost engaged once. He was the president of his fraternity at UVA."

Luc hated him already.

"He was blond and handsome, played on the university tennis team and was premed."

Hmmph. Luc was his team's medic and wasn't impressed by any pretty-boy doctor wannabe.

"We even got pinned."

"Pinned?" What was that? He thought he knew pretty much every slang word for sex out there.

She blushed, her face heating against his arm. "Yeah, he gave me his fraternity pin to wear. It's regarded as a precursor to an engagement ring."

"Oh." Like giving a girl your varsity jacket before heading out to the sock hop. A whole world still existed that hadn't moved much past the nineteen-fifties.

"Have you ever pinned a girl, Luc?" she asked innocently.

Only if that was a slang term for sex. "No, I wasn't in a fraternity. So what happened to him?" Hopefully a slow and painful death involving invertebrates in bodily orifices.

The corners of her mouth turned down. "He was a cheater," she admitted. "With at least one of my sorority sisters, maybe two. Janey learned about it and told me. I didn't want to believe her, but she never lies. He admitted it when I confronted him." She gave Luc a small smile. "He was the human equivalent of a foil-wrapped chocolate Easter bunny—bright and fancy on the outside, but hollow and waxy on the inside. Too much will make you sick."

Poor Claire was still going through sugar withdrawal. Luc wondered what kind of chocolate he would be. "You're well rid of someone like that," he said dismissively, but she had turned her face away. "What else?"

"He said he had needs, and I hadn't satisfied them."

"That's garbage, Claire!"

She looked up, startled. "What?"

"You heard me. He was looking for an excuse to cheat."

"Yes, I know, but I didn't have any experience and—"

"And it was his job to show you how to please

him—his job to please you." He ran his hand down her arm. "Did he ever please *you,* Claire? Ever make you scream his name in pure ecstasy? Ever take you so high you thought you'd never come down?"

"No, never." She was trembling against him now.

"Then he wasn't a man at all. And you please me plenty." He pulled her under him and proceeded to show her how much she pleased him—several times.

When they lay together, sweaty and satisfied again, he asked the question that had popped into his head earlier. "So what kind of chocolate am I, Claire?" he asked lazily.

"Chocolate? Hmm, let's see. You'd be dark, strong chocolate that melted on my tongue and made me crave more."

"And you would be a *petite* bonbon. Delicate, sweet, with a creamy soft center." As he was saying the words, they were sounding sentimental even to him, as if he were developing feelings for this woman. True, he did have feelings for her: respect and admiration for her tenacity, her kind nature, how the sun picked up caramel highlights in her hair and how her lips curved to showcase her white teeth...*non.* Respect and admiration on a purely professional level was best. That was all.

THE NEXT DAY, LUC handed her his satellite phone. "We've been out here four days. You should call someone to check in."

She accepted it reluctantly. Here in the woods was

their own little world, free from fathers and friends and family obligations. On the other hand, her father was quite capable of having one of his governor buddies call out the local National Guard to search for her.

Luc showed her how to work the phone. "Can they tell where I am?"

"No. One of our tech guys arranged it so the signal relays through several foreign countries. Unless they have access to Green Beret technology at the exact moment you call, they don't have a prayer of tracing us."

"Good." That made her feel marginally better. "Still, I think I'll call Janey." She dialed and had to smile when she heard Janey's cautious hello. Goodness only knew what was showing on her phone's caller ID.

"Janey, it's me, Claire."

After the relative peace of the woods, her friend's shriek jabbed through her head like a jackhammer. "Claire, oh, my God, where the hell are you? We're all going nuts here. I can't believe you went off in the woods with that guy. Are you okay? Your dad's about to call in bloodhounds and the FBI to find you even though he got your notes and voice mails."

"Janey, I'm fine," she answered, cutting through her friend's chatter. "I've had several days of survival training. Luc taught me how to clean and cook fish, rabbits and even snakes." She made a face.

"Wow," Janey said cautiously. "But, Claire, this isn't like you. I thought for sure you'd be back by now. You didn't even take three-quarters of your gear."

Claire fought down her anger. "Janey, my dad put GPS tracking devices in my stuff—my boots, my purse, my bags."

"Oh. That's a bit much, even for him."

"And he made all those arrangements for training me at Parris Island, having me sleep in the VIP hotel every night. Do you know what I've done out here? I built a sleeping platform out of real live trees with a real machete that I sharpened myself. I slept on it for two nights. And those were two long nights, Janey."

"Where have you slept the other nights, Claire?" her friend asked quietly.

"Once I proved I could do it, Luc let me off the hook and put up the tent he'd stashed."

"You know that's not what I'm asking."

"I know what you're asking and I'm not answering." She and Janey had always shared everything, but this thing with Luc was too raw and untested to giggle over with her friend. Not that Janey sounded in the mood to giggle.

"Roger that, Claire. What I don't know, I can't tell your father."

"Exactly. You can tell him I found his spies in the sky, and you can tell him that my survival training is on *my* terms." Luc raised his eyebrows at her emphatic conversation.

"Don't you think you should call him yourself to tell him? He is worried sick about you being alone in the woods with some stranger."

"He's not a stranger anymore."

"That's what I thought." Janey sighed. "When will you be back? *Where* will you be back? At least let me tell your dad that."

Claire considered that and nodded. "Let me check with Luc." She turned to him. "When are we coming back?"

He studied her for a second. "You want to go now?"

"No." She still had plenty to learn, about survival, as well as about Luc.

"Three days from now. We'll meet your father at the Special Forces compound at Bragg, where we first met."

She relayed the information to Janey.

"Okay, that will be the eleventh and plenty of time for you to pack for your flight."

"Oh, right." In the whole crucible of her experience, she had almost forgotten about leaving for the settlement at Río San Lucas.

"You are still going to South America, aren't you?" Janey's tone was dry. "That *is* the reason you're out in the woods eating snakes with a snake-eater."

"Honestly, Janey, 'snake-eater' isn't the nicest way to refer to Green Berets. Didn't Olie tell you that?"

"You don't even want to know what Olie told me." Her voice went from dry to pissed-off.

"Really? Well, you'll have to fill me in later. I don't want to run down the battery."

"I imagine not. According to my caller ID, you're calling from Uzbekistan. Quite the survival trip, that."

Claire finally had to laugh. "We're a bit closer than Uzbekistan, if my dad asks."

"Oh, he will, Claire. He will." With that foreboding prediction, they said their goodbyes.

Luc studied her face, his own unreadable. "She's worried about you?"

"Yeah," Claire admitted. "This is all pretty out of character for me."

"Me, too." He stared off into the woods. "Maybe I should have kept you at Parris Island. You still could have learned the basics."

She frowned at him. "How was I supposed to learn how to survive at night? How was I supposed to gut all those fish if I knew I had a hamburger and fries waiting for me for dinner? Hunger is a powerful motivator."

"I was hungry, too—hungry for you."

"Well, don't look so thrilled about it."

He wore a sourpuss expression. "I'm not happy. I'm letting my…need for you cloud my judgment. And clouded judgment gets people hurt."

"I won't get hurt."

"There's so much you need to know." He paced the clearing. "A proper course would take weeks, if not months."

She jumped in front of him. "But there are all those stories of people who survive terrible things without much or any formal training."

He crossed his arms in front of his chest. "And there are plenty of well-trained men who die anyway."

"So what's the point?" She made a sweeping gesture at the fire she had started with a flint and steel, the fish and game she had painstakingly cleaned, the water she had purified. "If none of this means a damn, why bother? If those big, tough men can't make it even with all their knowledge, I should curl into a ball and die if I ever get dumped in the middle of nowhere."

"Stop it!" He reached out and grabbed her arms, shaking her. "If you ever get into trouble, you will remember every damn thing I tell you and you will get your ass to safety. You are not going to die."

"Okay, Luc." She shook off his grip.

He stared at her and slumped onto a log, a stunned look on his face. "I'm so sorry. I shouldn't have touched you like that."

"No, you shouldn't have. Why did you?"

"'Cuz I can't stand the idea of you dying lost and alone—you dying, period." He rubbed his eyes. "I…well, I've lost teammates who seemed invincible."

She sat next to him. "Nobody is invincible. My mother lived in the jungle for over twenty years without any problems but then died from cancer." She slugged him in the biceps, definitely causing more damage to herself than him. "Oh, why am I lecturing you on danger, anyway? You jump out of planes, sneak around in enemy territory and probably go shark-hunting for fun in flippers with a knife clenched between your teeth. You are the last person to bitch at me about risk. Didn't you tell me you had a pet alligator when you were a kid?"

"Yeah." He finally grinned, showing her a couple round white scars on his forearm. "Li'l bastard got me good before I smartened up."

"Got rid of him?"

"No, got fast enough to avoid being bit. Once he got big enough to take an arm off, I let him loose in the swamp."

Claire sighed. "And you think I'm crazy for wanting to go teach some kids? Believe me, I'll stay away from the alligators."

"Okay, *béb*." He put his arm around her shoulders. "You're gettin' to be one tough chick. Maybe the gators'll swim away when they see you coming."

She laughed and leaned into his side. "You bet. They know I need a new alligator purse."

He laughed. "Since you're stickin' 'round for the end of training, I need to figure out what to cover next."

"What, you thought I'd quit before now?"

"That was before I knew you," he replied diplomatically.

"Since I've made it almost to the end, what comes toward the end of the training for a real Green Beret?"

"SERE training—survival, evasion, resistance and escape. SERE training is heavy duty and only a few soldiers can hack it. The rest wash out to their regular units."

"Oh. Are you going to teach me some SERE skills?"

"No way. You need months of training before you'd be even half-ready for that. I'm happy you know how to use a compass now."

Claire pursed her lips. She thought she'd done slightly better than that. "I bet you I can hide from you—at least for a while."

"*Cher,* you couldn't win a game of hide-and-seek with a two-year-old."

"Hey! You too chicken to try?"

He gave her an amused smile bordering on the edge of smirkiness. She hated when people smirked at her.

"I mean it. A big, bad Green Beret like you can't find a civilian out here? What kind of bayou boy are you?"

"Listen, I could track a mosquito through the air if I wanted. But I don't."

"What do you want?"

"You." He gave her a blatant stare that made her quiver, but not enough to back down.

"Well, you're not going to get me like that." She snapped her fingers. "You think I need more training— well, train me in this evasion stuff."

He rubbed his chin. "All right. You wanna do some evasion training, we'll do it. Gear up."

She quickly gathered her knife, compass, flashlight and canteen, strapping the machete in its scabbard to her waist. Its weight was comforting now rather than scary.

He examined her from head-to-toe, shaking his

head. "Damn, who'd have thought a woman could look so sexy wearing a machete."

"I'm full of surprises."

He gave her some last-minute instructions about avoiding snakes and gators. "Now the part that comes after evasion is resistance. When I catch you—"

"You mean 'if,'" she interrupted, trying for bravado.

"No, I don't. *When* I catch you, you are my captive and totally within my power. Under my absolute control."

"So what does that mean?"

"You have to do anything I want. Unless you want to resist me—you know, just for practice. That's the R in SERE. Resistance."

The part of being under his control sounded a bit menacing. Luc would never hurt her, but she wasn't tough enough to resist much.

He watched her closely. "You up for this?"

"Absolutely."

"I find you, you're mine. Every last inch of you. For as long as I say so."

She swallowed hard.

"I'll give you a half hour's head start. Enough time to get yourself away, but not too far lost. Ready?"

She nodded.

"Go."

She scurried out of camp, noting with irritation how he leaned against the log and tipped his hat over his eyes to take a catnap.

She'd show him. Her ancestors had hidden from the British and the Yankees both. Surely some of their abilities had been passed along. She stepped into the nearby stream, careful to not disturb any rocks to give away her moves.

Walking upstream was actually kind of pleasant, her poor, battered feet cooling after several minutes in the brackish water. The birds sang overhead and even that fat stick floating toward her was interesting.

Oh, no, that was a snake swimming downstream, not a stick. Well, that would be a real bite in the butt if she got snakebit. Claire stepped purposely to one side of the stream, trying not to scream and sprint from the water like she desperately wanted to. According to Luc, most snake species around here were non-venomous, except for two: rattlesnakes didn't swim and the other… The snake sensed the changing current and opened its white-lined mouth wide, its fangs a-popping.

This was the other venomous snake in the area—the cottonmouth. She gasped and froze, trying to gauge which way the snake would swim. *Away from me, away from me.*

LUC STARED AT CLAIRE'S retreating back through slitted eyes until she was out of sight. He jumped to his feet. A thirty minute head start? What was he, nuts? There were a thousand bad things that could happen to someone inexperienced in the woods.

He paced in the clearing for several seconds and grabbed his own canteen to go after her. No, wait. He stopped. He'd made a bet with her and he wasn't a cheater.

He started walking again. What was cheating compared to Claire's safety? He stopped again. But everyone was trying to keep her safe—that was the problem. Too safe for her own good. A baby bird who never dove from the nest had weak wings, easy prey for any chickenhawk that came after it. And much as he hated it, he wouldn't do her any favors by coddling her.

He checked his watch. Twenty-five minutes to wait. He had the feeling it might be the longest twenty-five minutes of his life.

THE CURRENT WAS SHOVING that snake right at her—she wouldn't escape the water in time and the snake could, of course, follow her up the bank. She looked around wildly for a stick or rock to chuck at its head, but no luck. A branch brushed her hair and she glanced up.

Was it thick enough to support her weight? Only one way to find out. She wrapped her hands around the rough bark and yanked. It didn't crack, so she swung her one leg up and then the other, struggling to lock her ankles together.

"Whoa!" Her backpack swung from her shoulders in a crazy arc and threatened to unbalance her. She glanced down and nearly fell into the water as the snake oscillated under her, gaping and hissing.

"No, no!" She dug what were left of her fingernails into the bark. His ghost-white mouth was even scarier close up, its fangs as long as her pinky finger. Why had she made that stupid bet with Luc? If he were here, he'd have probably killed it and cooked it by now. Instead she was going to be the snake's lunch.

After what seemed like an hour, the snake veered off and continued its reptilian way downstream.

And just in time because her arms and legs were about to give out. No more snakes in sight. She carefully lowered her feet into the stream and released the branch. Wincing, she examined the hunks of dirt and crud embedded in her skin and rinsed her hands. At least she wasn't bleeding too much. Once she found a stopping place, she'd disinfect the open cuts with her liquid hand sanitizer.

She walked upstream, her legs wobbling slightly from the adrenaline aftershock. Wow, she'd done it. She had saved herself from a nasty-looking snake. And all by herself. Maybe this survival stuff wasn't so bad.

But that didn't mean she'd won the bet. She glanced at her watch. Only five minutes before Luc started after her. She checked the riverbank for a place to step out of the water. She found a relatively flat grassy area that might not show her bootprints and hopped onto it.

Okay, now what? She saw a deeply wooded copse just past the grass and headed into the brushy part, careful not to break any branches. Luc had taught her the fresh green insides of broken wood were an obvious giveaway. She was really glad she'd worn long pants or else Luc would have been able to track the blood from her scratched legs. She didn't need any more injuries.

Geez, it was nice and cool in here, at least ten degrees cooler than in the open. Claire took the time to suck in a refreshing breath. But not too much time. Luc would move much faster than she did, especially with her snake delay.

Oh, a big tree with a hollow at its base was inside the grove. Claire picked up a stick and poked the leaf litter. Nothing came leaping out at her, so she decided to give that a try. The entrance was fairly overgrown but she still needed some camouflage.

Luckily there was a big pile of freshly fallen tree branches whose leaves had started to wilt. She shoved them in front of the hollow, climbed in and pulled her wooden screen closed.

Claire looked up. She'd never been inside a tree before. She had about eight inches of clearance above her head. She'd never been claustrophobic, so it was more cozy than enclosed. Her hidey-hole had kind of a musty, dry smell but wasn't unpleasant. She tried not to think of what kind of crud was lurking below the dry leaves underneath her.

Maybe she should clean her hands before they got infected. She manually picked out the last bark bits and pulled out her pocket hand sanitizer. She bit back a gasp as the rubbing alcohol hit raw flesh. Wow, that hurt. Waving her hands in the enclosed space, she wondered how long she would need to stay to prove her point. It wasn't as if Luc would stand in the middle of the woods and yell, "Ollie, Ollie, oxen-free" or "Come out, come out, wherever you are." She might need to spend the night in the tree. She hadn't considered that when she made the bet. But if she lost, she was his captive. Under his total control. For as long as he wanted.

So why wasn't Claire jumping out and calling his name?

Because this wasn't some sexy hide-and-seek game she was playing—this was a test of her skills and endurance.

It sure was quiet and cool inside here. She yawned. Between hard physical work during the day and heavy duty sex with Luc at night, she hadn't gotten much sleep all week. She rested her head on her bent knees. Maybe she'd close her eyes for just a minute.

8

LUC GAZED DOWN AT Claire sleeping soundly in her tree. She'd given it a good try, but he'd found overturned rocks and some bent blades of grass where she'd entered and exited the stream. Once he'd hit the clearing, he'd smelled the rubbing alcohol in her hand sanitizer, and that was it for her.

He wavered for a minute. Maybe he should let her off the hook, pretend she'd tricked him.

But if she didn't learn from her mistakes, why the hell was he training her? Would an enemy let her off the hook? No.

He bent down and clamped a heavy hand on her ankle. She let out a scream.

"Gotcha." Luc purposely hardened his expression, became a stranger.

"Yeah, you got me. How did you find me?" She wiggled out of the hollow and screamed again as he tossed her over his shoulder.

He ignored her question. "You gonna come easy or do I have to tie you up?"

"Tie me up?" she squeaked, his shoulder probably

pressing into her diaphragm. "Oh, no, you don't." She struggled against him, kicking her boots into his thighs and almost landing one where it counted.

He set her on her feet, careful to keep a mean look on his face. "I hunted you, I found you, and you're my captive now."

"What? No, that was a joke, right?" He pulled out a length of rope and tied her wrists together. "Luc!" She finally tried resisting and swung her hands at his head, which he easily ducked, tying her ankles together, as well.

He swung her onto his shoulder again and headed for camp. "You wanted SERE training, you got it. You survived for an hour, but your evasion and resistance leave something to be desired. As for escape, we'll see about that." Once he had her in the tent, she wouldn't be out of his sight.

"Hey, I did more than survive, I won that part." Her breath was choppy due to his quick pace. "Did you see that gigantic cottonmouth swimming downstream?"

"Yeah, why?" It had been a big son of a bitch. Used to them, Luc hadn't thought twice about it.

"It came straight at me. Fangs and all."

"What?" He slowed for a second. She hadn't been bit, had she? He picked up the pace to carry her to camp and his snakebite kit.

"But I escaped it." She gasped for air again. "Grabbed a branch…swung my legs up. Went right under me." She slammed his ass with her hands. "So there."

Good for her. He shivered for a second. What if she'd been bitten and he hadn't found her? She could have gotten seriously ill.

He forced himself not to soften. But she hadn't been bitten, and maybe some of her success was due to his training. Her wings were getting stronger.

"What…gave me away?"

Good, she wanted to know so she didn't make the same mistake. "You overturned a couple rocks, crushed some grass, but that stinky hand sanitizer was a dead giveaway."

"Crap," she muttered.

Luc allowed himself a grin since she couldn't see his face. To tell the truth, he was enjoying this walk with her curvy butt next to his cheek, her breasts rubbing his back. He ran his hand up her thighs and she let out a yelp.

"What are you doing?"

"Checking my prisoner for weapons."

"Don't have any there…you ass."

He wasn't sure. To him, her body was one deadly weapon as far as he was concerned. "You gonna honor our bet? Or weasel out?"

"What'd you have…in mind?" She sounded nervous but a bit excited, as well.

"*Oui ou non,* Claire?" Shoot, he shouldn't have used her first name. That made him seem like an easy mark.

"Yes, all right!"

Good. She was all his to do what he wanted to do. He'd make sure she enjoyed herself, as well, since watching her come was so fuckin' sexy.

A few minutes later, Luc approached their camp. "Ah, we're home." He dumped her onto the sleeping bag and she glared up at him.

"I suppose that little caveman stunt of yours made you all hot and bothered?" Her tone was frosty but he sensed the same excitement building in her.

"Sure did, *cher.*" Her breasts were bobbing up and down against her shirt. "I think I'm gon' make you all hot and bothered, too."

"Untie me." She held out her wrists imperiously for him to loosen her.

"Fine. But there'll be no escape for you." He cut her hands free, but quickly pushed her onto the bedding.

"Luc, what are you doing?" she all but squealed.

He'd been aggressive with plenty of bad guys and even a couple bad ladies, but they'd never brought out this almost animalistic lust that Claire was inspiring in him.

"You ever let a man do whatever he wanted with you, sweet Claire?" She shook her head. He hadn't thought so. "You never trusted any of them enough for that, did you?" She looked away but he read the truth in her eyes. "You trust me?"

She looked at him with her big brown eyes and nodded. His heart gave an extra beat. Her trust was beginning to mean the world to him. "I want to do all sorts of wicked, naughty things to you while you're like this, Claire."

Her pupils dilated and she gasped. Bingo.

He licked the shell of her ear and sucked on the lobe, sending shivers through her. "You want this, *oui ou non?*" he murmured. "You tell me *'oui,'* then no stopping." To seal the deal, he nuzzled her neck, where her pulse beat furiously.

She nodded slowly. *"Oui."*

"Now you belong to me." His blood pounded through his veins at the idea of making her totally his. "Say it."

"I belong to you," she whispered.

Damn right. His cock immediately hardened at her capitulation. He sat on his haunches and ran his hands leisurely over her clothed body. Breasts, belly, bottom. Down the outside of her legs and up the inside. He wiggled his hand between her thighs and pressed it to the searing heat between. Oh, yes, here was the proof that sweet Mademoiselle Claire was totally turned on by his game.

She gasped as he leisurely pressed the heel of his hand on her center. "Oh, Luc, there."

He immediately withdrew his touch. "You don't have any say, remember? You are only here to give me pleasure." That wasn't true, but it sounded good.

"Yes, Luc." She bit her lip with her white teeth and he nearly groaned himself.

He straddled her thighs, his erection resting right below her belly button. He unbuttoned her shirt, revealing her white cotton bra, two points pushing eagerly at the fabric. She lay quietly but watchfully, waiting to see what he would do next. Next was the front clasp of her bra, easily flicked open. He spread the cups apart and she was bare to the waist.

He would never get tired of seeing her plump breasts topped with sweet milk-chocolate nipples. They tightened even further under his hungry gaze. She instinctively tried to cover herself, but he wouldn't let her.

Instead she met his gaze defiantly. Good. He didn't want to break her spirit. He deliberately covered her breasts with his hands, thumbing her nipples. She tried to stifle a little moan, but that small sound sent a wave of triumph over him.

"You have pretty tits. Too soft and sweet for a rough man like me." He bent down and gently rubbed his cheek over her soft, soft skin, his stubble grazing her nipples. Her heartbeat strummed in his ear, a near match to his.

Despite his desire, he took his time, sucking on one peak as he toyed with the other. They swelled under his fingers and tongue as Claire's whimpers spurred him on. "Ah, you love this?" He didn't need any answer to know she did like what he was doing—the bucking of her hips giving her away.

He dragged his tongue lazily around her left breast,

looking into her hazy brown eyes before blowing a stream of cold air across her wet flesh.

"Luc!" She wiggled against him.

"Quiet!" he commanded. "Or else I'm gon' roll you onto your belly and give you a good spanking."

Damned if her hips didn't buck again, the idea arousing her and him, as well, as he imagined his hand on her bare ass, hearing her yelps of mixed pleasure and pain. He wiped his damp forehead. She was turning him into a real pervert.

He swung off her body and undid her pants, pulling them and her panties down to her ankles. She let her knees fall open, showing him everything. His nostrils flared at her scent. He'd been dying to taste for himself, but she'd been too shy.

Not anymore. He was in charge, right? Right. He stripped off her boots and clothing. Was she ever sexy, her breasts thrusting into the air, her slim waist curving into round, full hips and tapering into strong, sexy legs. Even her peach-painted toenails made him hard. *"Je vais te lécher le clito, toi."*

"You're going to lick my what?" She lifted her head, only to drop it as he put action to words and licked her hard clit for all he was worth. Now the hip bucking really began, forcing him to clamp his arms around her thighs to keep his face in her burning-hot *chatte*.

He was as hungry as if he'd come out of a six-week training exercise and she was a lavish buffet. He couldn't get enough of her salty-sweet taste, her musky smell, her silky thighs locking around his head. She was probably screaming but he couldn't hear so well. Her body told him plenty, though, her juices slicking his face. He darted his tongue over her clit, her pussy, even plunging deep inside her like a little cock.

Luc moaned into her body, imagining his big cock doing the same. Who was being tormented here, anyway? She shuddered under him, and he slipped two fingers inside her pussy and found a swollen nub on the wall. He pressed gently and she went wild, thrusting and arching until she came, shouting his name.

Claire finally calmed and Luc let her go, kneeling over her naked body again. "You never did that before, did you, *cher?*"

She shook her head, her face flushed and sweaty.

"Good." A primal satisfaction rushed through his veins, his adrenaline pumping as if he'd completed a successful mission. He had been the first. He stood and eagerly stripped off his T-shirt, pants and boots. His underwear was the last and most welcome to go.

Standing naked and erect over her sated form, he was a conqueror about to plunder her body. He'd introduced her to the joys of a thorough orgasm, made her scream in delight, and now it was his turn.

"What are you going to do now, Luc?"

"It's your turn to pleasure me now."

CLAIRE STARED AT HIM, still limp and sweaty from Luc's demanding mouth. She knew her face was red, and she hoped he thought it was from her climax instead of embarrassment. She'd always declined that particular act, and her boyfriends had probably been grateful, eager to get onto the main act.

But everything with Luc was the main act. She'd never imagined any sensations like the ones he'd demanded with that mouth, those lips, that tongue—even his teeth. He even might have bit her gently at one point.

That had been the best climax ever, and now it was his turn. She spread her legs wide, waiting for him to sheathe himself inside her. Maybe she could come again if he played with her.

Instead, he straddled her waist, careful to keep his weight off her, his powerful thighs bunching with the effort. His heavy penis rested on her stomach, his male sac tickling her skin. Instead of moving down her body, though, he moved up.

Leaning forward to rest his hands on either side of her head, he began thrusting, deliberately rubbing himself all over her breasts. His skin was soft and silky and hot—so very hot. He left a trail of slippery fluid on her skin, marking her as his. She never knew anything like this was possible as he drew circles around her nipples with his penis, making her hips wiggle under him again.

The pressure between her legs built, but Luc didn't show any inclination to hurry, no tendency to push inside her and relieve his own desire.

"Luc?" she asked. His eyes were closed, his breath coming quickly.

He opened his eyes. "What are you willing to do to please me, my captive?"

Her answer was immediate. "Anything."

"Bien. Léche-moi." He delicately brushed her lips with the tip of his erection, commanding her to lick him. Claire stared at him, her eyes wide. She knew if she'd refused, Luc would not force her, but she was deep in their fantasy and didn't want to leave it. She'd never done this before, either, but tonight was a night for firsts.

She opened her mouth hesitantly and he glided in, hot and salty inside her. He moved slowly in and out as she got used to the taste and feel of him. She flicked her tongue over his tip to taste him better and he groaned. He was burning hot, slick and salty.

Encouraged by his response, she relaxed her lips and let him sink deeper, her mouth learning his swells and contours, from the juicy, plump head topping his long, thick shaft. She was amazed she had managed to fit all of him before. Of course, coming three or four times tended to make that part easier.

His muscles were straining, and he was fighting the urge to take her roughly. She decided to play with him and sucked gently on him. He shivered, and she allowed herself a smile around him.

"Oui, bébé, oui, oui." He picked up the pace, her mouth caressing and sucking his swollen flesh.

Claire couldn't believe how exciting it was to have his powerful body moving over her. She felt powerful, too, his face contorting with his effort at restraint.

She had no such restraint. He had started this game of sex, and she was going to finish it. Now that she knew her power over this man, he was toast. She remembered a little bit of sexual trivia from Janey and hummed as she firmly sucked down on him.

He yelped, a burst of fluid coating her tongue. "No, Claire. Let me go, or I'll…I'll…" His words were interspersed with groans.

Shaking her head slightly, she ignored his pleas and licked him some more. He tried to pull out, but she sucked hard on him until he moaned. "Ah, my sweet…Claire… I'm gonna…come."

Claire gave a hidden smile of satisfaction and daringly scraped her teeth over his supersensitive shaft. Luc shouted his release, calling her name as he exploded into her throat. Claire inhaled deeply and swallowed his hot juices. It was amazing how sex with this man was so different than any other.

He finally stopped shuddering and withdrew, his arms and legs shaking as he dropped into a seated position on the sleeping bags, his back to her.

Claire stared at his bowed spine. Why wouldn't he look at her? Had she done it wrong? He'd definitely enjoyed himself. Maybe she'd hurt him, using her teeth like that. Or maybe he thought less of her for forcing him to finish like that. Maybe only bimbos let men do *that* to them. She blinked hard. Enough of this kinky stuff. She was obviously bad at it. "Luc? Did I do something wrong?"

LUC STARTED AT HER tentative voice. Of course—she wasn't used to this kind of sex game. He turned around. *Mon Dieu,* she was fighting back tears. Calling himself all sorts of bad names, he pulled her into his arms.

She stretched a bit, her breasts and hips wiggling in unconscious sensuality. Holy crap, he was fifteen kinds of horn-dog to even want to take her all over again right now. "You okay?" He hoped she'd think his erection was left over and not brand-new.

"Fine." She struggled into a seated position, her dark hair swinging in front of her face so he couldn't read her expression.

"Um, Claire, was that too much for you?"

"Of course not." He wasn't sure, but her laugh sounded fake. "It's just, I've never done…" She trailed off.

"Oh, of course not." Awkward, anyone? "Um, me neither." But he wanted to do it again. "Did you enjoy yourself?"

The visible curve of her cheek flushed. "Yes," she whispered.

Growing bolder, he cupped her chin and tipped her face to his. She avoided his gaze. "I enjoyed myself, too—you know that, don't you?"

"You did?" She looked at him in surprise. "I thought I hurt you."

"You? How could you hurt me?"

"With, um, my teeth." Her last two words were an embarrassed whisper.

Luc swallowed hard and got even harder. Her teeth scraping along his cock had thrown him bodily over the edge. "No. That was really sexy. Did I hurt you, kneeling over you, pushing into your mouth?"

She shook her head. "No. It made me feel... powerful." She finally met his glance. "Like I was the one in charge despite the circumstances." Her nipples were tightening again.

He stroked her cheek, running his hand down her slim neck to her fine collarbone. "You were in charge, *ma belle. Totalement* in charge of me. And I know you liked it when I licked your little *clito.*"

He helped her gently lay back down on the sleeping bags. He lay next to her, caressing her breasts.

"Yes." She breathed faster. "I loved it." She buried her face in his shoulder.

"Next time, though, you need to ask me for it. I'll teach you some French you never learned in class. Ready?"

She nodded.

"*'Léche-moi le clito, mon cher.'*" Her face heated against his skin. "Come on, it makes me hot to hear you say what you want."

"*Baise-moi, mon cher.*" Her words were muffled but

perfectly understandable. His eyebrows flew up. He doubted she had ever invited a man to fuck her before, but he was more than willing to be the first invitee.

"You got it, sweetheart." Without another word, he reached into his bag for protection and positioned himself between her thighs.

She wrapped her arms around his neck and he slid inside her. They both sighed, her eyes closing. She was tight and still wet from before and he fought to keep from coming again. He'd never been like this before, so eager with a woman that he lost control almost immediately.

She began moving under him, and he fell into a steady rhythm, dipping deep into her and pulling out until only his head stayed inside. She clutched at his shoulders, her breath singeing his skin. Mindful of their walk on the wild side, he kept it slow but she wouldn't stand for it, wrapping her legs around his hips and grinding into him, her hot, sweet pussy surrounding his cock in a luxurious prison. Ah, who was the captive now?

"Baise-moi plus, mon cher," she repeated, urging him to fuck her more. He gave up and slammed into her, plucking at her diamond-hard clit.

After that, she didn't say anything except his name, called over and over again. She spasmed around him, an orgasmic flush climbing her glistening breasts to her beautiful face. Her mouth fell open as she gasped. He didn't let up on the finger pressure and she moaned, coming a second time.

She dug her fingers into his ass, and he dropped to his elbows, twisting and writhing on top of her, around her, in her, telling her all sorts of nasty, naughty things he planned to do to her the next time. Tie her up, tie her down, spank her, lick her, spank her while he licked her, spank her while he fucked her...

To his more-than-pleasant surprise, Claire shook and squeezed around him a third time, her head tipped back and her mouth open in a wordless scream.

He threw his own head back in a yell of pure triumph and pistoned into her pulsing heat. His yell turned into a groan as he emptied himself into her welcoming body again. Coming again after such a short time threatened to blow the top of his head off, and he was so wild he barely stayed inside her. She clung limply to him until he pulled out of her with a groan.

"Luc, Luc." Her voice was hoarse by now. "I never knew..."

He had never known anything like that, either. "I know, I know." He cleaned himself quickly and pulled her into his arms, his mind whirling. His emotions had run the gamut today, from worry to triumph to this odd mix of lust and tenderness.

And soon the woman of his dreams would fly south to the place of his nightmares.

"How are your feet doing, Claire?" Luc looked up from the gear he was packing.

She wiggled them experimentally. The raw patches had healed and she'd double-padded them today. "Pretty good, why?"

"I want to work on your map-reading skills." He pulled out a paper rectangle and spread out a topographical map.

Claire looked at the squiggles cautiously. It was very different from a forest or highway map, showing what Luc called "contour lines" to delineate the ups and downs of the land. There were also roads, bridges and electrical transmission lines, handy info for men like Luc who probably blew those up overseas. "What do I do?"

"We're here." His finger landed squarely on a spot next to a river.

"Really? Are you sure?"

He grinned. "I've known exactly where we've been the whole time. Why? You thought we were wandering around lost?"

She bit her lip. "Well…"

"Trust me—we're here. I want you to get us there." He pointed to a second tiny dot.

"What's there?" She peered at the dot. "Broomsburg? Is that a town?"

"More like a wide spot in the road—the only populated settlement in this area." He handed her a compass. "Which way do we go?"

Taking a deep breath, she watched the needle spin and settle facing north. She turned the map so that pointed north, as well, and peered at its layout. Taking a deep breath, she pointed to her right. "We go east."

He raised an eyebrow. "You sure?"

She looked at the map and the compass again. "We're here?"

"*Oui.*"

"And we want to go here?"

"*Oui.*"

"It's east. Let's go."

"Yes, ma'am." He snapped a salute. She bet he looked hotter than hot in his uniform. Well, it was unlikely she'd ever see that, wasn't it?

She folded the map so she could see the pertinent area and made sure she had enough water for a hike. It was fun to be in charge for once. Goodbye to the girl who had wandered the mall parking lot for almost two hours.

They walked steadily for about an hour, Claire making minor course corrections according to the map. She stopped and bit her lip when they came to a river that wasn't on the map. Had she taken them the wrong way? She double-checked their route but everything looked right.

"What is it?"

"The river—it doesn't belong here."

"Somebody forgot to tell it that." Luc stared at the sluggish brown water.

What should she do? She looked where they'd come from and hesitated.

"Make a decision, Claire. Forward or backward?"

Enough backtracking. She knew she was right and the river was wrong. Or the map was wrong. It was created by people, after all, and people made mistakes sometimes. "Forward. But we should cross at the narrowest point since we don't know how deep it is in the middle."

"Lay on, Macduff," he quoted in a perfect Scottish accent.

"Don't tell me you performed in *Macbeth*, too. And I thought it was 'Lead on, Macduff.'"

"Bad luck to say that play's name, *béb*. Better calling it the Scottish play. And no, that's the correct phrase."

"What part did you have?"

"The title role."

Claire shook her head. Luc Boudreaux would never be second fiddle to anyone. "Let's go. And while we walk, you can tell me if your Lady Macbeth was scary in real life." She picked her way down the riverbank.

"Hoo-wee, was she ever. That actress dabbled in hoodoo and claimed she called up dark spirits during her mad scene. All I know was she made the hairs stand up on the back of my neck. What can I say? There are plenty of strange things in the world."

"Like me running around in the woods?"

"You're doing a great job, Claire. I should have told you before, but I'm not used to giving compliments to the men I train. You've done better than some of them."

She smiled to herself. "Thank you." It was a great compliment, considering how little she'd known before setting off on their adventure together. She stopped and grabbed his hand.

"What?" He immediately scanned the woods for danger. "Did you see something?"

"Nope, just you." Impulsively, she stood on her tip-toes and pressed a kiss on his firm lips.

"Me, huh?" He returned her kiss, drawing her tight against him. The river rushed next to them, but not hard enough to drown out the roaring in her ears. His mouth was warm and wet, and he kissed her leisurely, as if they were sitting on a park bench with all the time in the world. She stroked the rugged line of his jaw with her free hand, and he turned his face to kiss her palm.

Her eyes flew open. His display of tenderness had surprised him, too, judging from how his black eyes widened before his customary cool mask dropped into place.

Claire turned back to her map, confused. She thought she was the only one who was fighting off feelings of affection, but if Luc started returning her feelings, she was sunk. Once in San Lucas, she could manage a wistful memory of the "one who got away," but if he *did* want to chase her, she was pretty sure she'd let herself be caught.

But that couldn't be her focus right now. She had to laugh. Here they were in some swampy woods that looked like a t-rex habitat, and her hard-as-nails Special Forces trainer was quoting Shakespeare to her. "So, you're a Shakespearean actor. Now you have to perform your favorite Shakespeare speech for me."

He hesitated for a second. "I've never performed this role before."

"Do I look like a drama critic?" She was carefully placing one foot after another to avoid slipping in the mud along the river. "Which one?"

"Okay. It's King Henry the Fifth of England rallying his outnumbered men before the Battle of Agincourt in 1415." He took a deep breath and started the monologue about how the valor of his soldiers would cause the entire kingdom to remember the battle and curse the fact they had not fought for England.

By the time he had reached the end, tears ran down Claire's cheeks and the path was a brown blur in front of her eyes. She swallowed hard several times before speaking. "'We few, we happy few, we band of brothers…'" she quoted, surreptitiously wiping her eyes. "I never knew where that quote came from."

"The St. Crispin's Day Speech. Really shows what it meant to lead men—Henry led by the strength of his conviction and the force of his personality."

"Is that how you feel? That you and your team are a band of brothers?"

"Absolutely." Not a trace of doubt entered his tone. "'For he to-day who sheds his blood with me shall be my brother.' I am their brother and they are mine. I would die for them and they would die for me. Some have, matter of fact."

No wonder there was little room for her—little room for any woman in his life. She needed to remember that before she did something stupid like fall in love with the man. It would be so easy to do—the way his rare smiles grew more frequent, the way his hand lingered on her as he helped her to her feet, the way he looked at her when he thought she wouldn't notice.

They would both return to their separate duties once the week was over. She would fly to South America and he would fly somewhere secret in another desperate region of the world.

She didn't know what to say, so she focused on the river now that her eyes were clear. It had narrowed to a point where she could see the rocky bottom. "Maybe we should cross here." She fiddled with the compass, unsure where the heck she even was.

Luc was silent behind her, not moving or giving her any hints. She remembered how old King Henry had led and summoned some hidden force of personality. "We cross here." Not waiting for Luc to agree or confirm her decision, she stepped into the cool water.

He followed her across without comment. She checked the map to reorient herself from the slight detour they'd taken and started walking again.

It wasn't until about ten minutes later that he

spoke. "Hurricane Inez came through several years ago. The flooding cut several new river channels. That was one of 'em."

"Oh." She spun to face him and whacked him in the chest with the map. "You gave me an old map? No fair! What kind of trick is that?"

"Did you check the date on the map?" He pointed to the corner.

She peered at the copyright. "1992. Oh."

"Never trust anyone else's gear. If you have to borrow, check it out first."

"Is Broomsburg still there? Or were its inhabitants driven away by the eruption of a long-dormant volcano that doesn't show up on this map, either?" She shook the paper at him.

He laughed and laughed. "Claire, you say the funniest things. Yeah, Broomsburg is still there and we need to get there. Take the point."

"Point of what?"

"Take the lead. 'Take the point' is army lingo for 'Lead the way.'"

"Fine." She looked at the map that was old enough to earn its driver's license and set off again. Still irritated, she was likely stomping through the woods slightly harder than necessary.

"Claire?" Luc's voice called.

"What?"

"You did fine. Thought on your feet like a real survivor. You can be my point man anytime."

"Thanks." A warm glow spread over her that had little to do with the sweltering heat.

"SO THIS IS BROOMSBURG?" Claire viewed the ramshackle collection of trailers and shacks with dismay.

"Congratulations, *cher*. You passed."

Not that visiting here was much of a prize. "It looks abandoned to me."

"People do live here." Luc pointed out several clues. "Satellite dishes on the roof, fat chickens running around and that pickup."

The monster red pickup truck was almost as nice as Luc's and probably cost more than ten of the dwellings—she couldn't bring herself to call them houses. "Do they even have indoor plumbing?"

He pointed to a hut tucked into the clearing's edge. "Easier to do your business outside than bother with a septic tank and all."

An outhouse. Ugh. And she thought peeing under a tree was bad. What the smell from that building must be…at least they were upwind.

A screen door smacked open on a pea-green metal trailer next to the red pickup. "What y'all doin' here?"

Luc smoothly swiveled her behind him. The speaker was a small woman, elderly, with slightly hunched shoulders.

"Hey. We just hikin' by on the way to the state park." He had purposely broadened his accent into deep Cajun.

"Y'all ain't from around here, that's fo' sho." She eyed Luc suspiciously.

"From de bayou, *cher.* On a li'l honeymoon."

The woman raised an eyebrow. "What kinda crazy honeymoon is that?" She peered at Claire. "You sho' 'bout marryin' a man who take you to Broomsburg for a honeymoon?"

"We ran away from my daddy and don't want him to find us."

She cackled. "Don't worry none 'bout that. He never find you here. Nobody can."

And that was starting to worry Claire.

She clutched Luc's arm in what she hoped looked like newlywed affection. Just as she was about to drag him away, a little figure peered out the door. "Is it Momma?"

"No, Callie."

"What a pretty name." Claire looked closer at the young girl with pink cheeks and mop of dusty blond hair. "How old is she?"

"Five."

"Almost old enough for school." Claire smiled at the child.

"We'll see. School cain't keep teachers long 'nuff to stay open. Maybe jus' teach her at home."

Claire didn't know what to say to that. She had nothing against homeschooling, but it was obvious that educational resources were sorely lacking here. "Well, good luck."

A loud snore came from the trailer and the woman started.

Luc caught Claire's elbow and steered her away. "You take care, ma'am."

Callie and the woman disappeared into the trailer and Luc and Claire disappeared into the woods. Luc took the point this time and set a blistering pace.

It wasn't until about forty-five minutes later that he finally called a halt to the forced march. Claire dropped onto a log and sucked down most of her canteen. "Want to tell me what happened?"

Luc's face was set in harsh lines. "I didn't want to stick around to meet the man of the house, *béb*. Could be he was bad news."

"Like what, a criminal?"

"Who knows?"

Claire cast an anxious glance over her shoulder. "What kind of crime?"

"Maybe drugs—pot or meth, likely. Could even be he's an orchid poacher. Collectors pay crazy amounts for illegally harvested, wild-grown plants."

"Really? Orchids? That sounds bizarre."

He urged her to her feet again. "Same here as in San Lucas de la Selva. Poor people, uneducated people don't have the same choices, some turn to crime."

"Yeah, and some don't." Claire glared at him. "Were you poor growing up?"

"Family of nine, living in the middle of nowhere? Hell, yeah, we was poor. Never went hungry 'cuz Papa knew how to hunt and fish, but poor."

"And you had the same choice. Did you turn to crime?"

He shook his head. "My papa never hesitated to pass me a slap if I needed it. After all those girls, he wasn't 'bout to let his only son go bad, disgrace the Boudreaux name. Now let's go. We're breaking camp and moving soon as we get back." He took off walking again.

"Don't you want the map?"

"That ol' thing?" He grinned at her. "I curved our path around so we should hit camp in another hour or so."

"Oh." Claire sagged briefly before following him. Another hour. Well, better that than being tracked by insane rural drug pushers. On the other hand, Luc didn't seem worried, just cautious. He probably wouldn't be worried if a hundred guys were tracking him in the woods, instead of one woman limping after him.

Claire desperately wished she had someone to talk to about her growing feelings for Luc. Until now, she'd always had Janey or one of her sorority sisters to pore over every detail of her relationships. She supposed it was a bit junior-high, but then again, her previous relationships had been juvenile, as well—unlike the unnerving sensations Luc provoked in her.

Janey would tell her to enjoy Luc without giving herself up to him, but Claire had a sneaking suspicion Janey had never been with a man like Luc.

9

CLAIRE SCANNED THEIR new camp the next afternoon.
Luc had moved them upriver and well away from
Broomsburg, telling her better safe than sorry.

She actually preferred this setup. The river had
carved out a natural swimming hole, away from the
main current, where the water was relatively clear.
They'd had an extremely fun skinny dip last night with
the stars and moon shining above.

Then up came the sun. Her tender lover left and her
hard-driving instructor returned. Today had been easier
than their massive hike yesterday due to her feet giving
her trouble, so he'd lectured her in depth on safe plants
versus poisonous ones. Claire remembered every word
with apprehension. Plants with milky sap were bad,
wild mushrooms were bad, white berries were bad—
heck, even the plant that made the deadly poison ricin
grew wild in the jungle. He'd carried along a field
identification guide to show her and after a while, all
the plants started to look the same—green and deadly.
Larva and frogs were looking mighty tasty after that
lesson.

Once she'd bathed, Claire stretched out on a towel on the wide rocks surrounding the watering hole. She didn't want to do any more survival training. Not because she was tired, or lazy, but because she wanted to spend the rest of their time making love.

Unfortunately, Luc had other ideas. He was pushing her training harder and harder, trying to cram every bit of knowledge he had into her head as their time together drew to a close. All of a sudden, it was four days before she was to leave for San Lucas, and he'd promised to return her to Ft. Bragg tomorrow, three days before her plane took off.

Only one day left with Luc. At the moment, she was having a hard time remembering why she wanted to go live in Snakeland, South America, when she could stay in the States with Luc. Then she remembered: he'd never asked her to stay in the first place.

What did she have to do, beg the man? She stifled a giggle. She had certainly enjoyed it. What else did he have to show her? He had an almost unlimited repertoire of sexual tricks up his sleeve, but the one that was making her really hot thinking about it was the one he had mentioned but not tried.

Quickly, before he came along, she stripped off her clean clothing and rearranged herself to lie naked on her stomach. She'd never sunbathed naked before, but that was small potatoes compared to her other new experiences.

Her head was cradled on her arms as if she were resting, but she knew the instant he saw her. Mostly because he shouted her name.

"What the hell are you doing lying there naked?"

She rolled onto her side nonchalantly, pleased to see his agog expression. "Sunbathing, what else?" She ran a hand down her hip. "No swimsuit lines this way."

"Swimsuit lines? I never heard anything so asinine. If you were a soldier under my command, I'd—"

Claire interrupted his rant with a yawn. "I thought I was under your command. Your *every* command," she said significantly, eying the growing bulge under his zipper. "It's your job to make sure I learn my lessons, but I don't see that happening," she said with a sniff.

He stood there in shock until comprehension dawned. "Claire, do you want me to punish you?" His voice became silky and menacing.

She was starting to feel aroused. She shrugged. "What? Make me do push-ups?"

"Nothing so ordinary as that. Lie on your stomach."

Oh, boy, what had she started now? But she did as he told her, hearing the clinks and thuds of his clothing and gear drop to the ground. She was practically quivering in happy anticipation by the time he knelt behind her and shoved a makeshift pillow of their clothing under her cheek.

She folded her arms out in front of her and rested her chin on them.

"Don't move. A bad girl like you needs to learn how to listen."

Ooh, she wiggled a bit but stopped when his big hand slapped her bottom.

"Ouch!"

"Quiet." But he massaged the stinging spot all the same.

"But what did I do wrong?"

He spanked her other cheek, just like she'd hoped when she asked the question. The sting jolted her a bit, but felt surprisingly good. "You knew I'd come here and find you naked, didn't you?"

"Yes," she whispered. Another smack.

"And you knew I couldn't resist the sweet curves of your ripe ass sticking up in the air."

"Yes." This time it was a bit harder, but still good.

"In fact, you've been flaunting your sexy little body to me ever since I came to your hotel room. You wanted me to rip off that nightgown and show you who was boss." *Smack.* "Do you know how close you came to bending over that big soft bed with my dick rammed inside you?"

She shook her head, her cheeks brushing her upper arms. "How close?"

"This close." His erection brushed her stinging bottom. "I could have done anything I wanted to you, and you would have begged me for more."

"Yes, Luc." She would have eagerly slept with him that night, even though he'd been a stranger.

"And I saw you bathing in the moonlight and saw you naked for the first time—your high, tight tits, your sweet, creamy pussy."

He'd spied on her in the woods? She'd been thinking about him as she slowly washed herself with the cloth, almost giving in to the impulse to touch herself.

"Did you know I started touching myself? Your little peep show almost made me shoot my load. But I held off until you begged me to fuck you."

And it was the best decision she'd ever made. But in the spirit of the game… "I'm sorry, Luc."

"Are you?" Three quick taps. "I think you're getting off on your punishment, Claire." She gasped as he delved between her thighs. "Oh, you are. Your pussy is dripping wet without me touching you." He withdrew his hand.

"More, more." She wiggled her hips against the towels, but he clamped down with both big hands.

"You'll get more when I let you." He pressed a column of moist openmouthed kisses from the nape of her neck, between her shoulder blades, down the small of her back. She gasped as he nuzzled her stinging bottom. "Only bad girls let men do all sorts of nasty things to them. Are you a bad girl, Claire?"

"I'll do anything you want right now." An eager, greedy tone had crept into her voice.

"Good." He prodded her with his erection and she instinctively widened her legs. "Take me, Claire." Without waiting for her reply, he filled her completely.

They moaned in unison, locked together. "Take me, Luc," she echoed.

He slid in and out of her, nudging the deepest parts of her. She arched her hips, daring him to speed up. "That's it, *cher.*" He curved over her as his hard abs rubbed her bottom.

Luc reached under her belly and found her swollen pleasure point. Claire cried out as he plucked at her. With half-groaned words of encouragement, he stroked her to the edge of her release. She writhed against the towel.

"Come on, *béb,* scream for me. I wan' hear you call my name." He nipped at her neck just like the stallion he'd called himself the other day. His big body dominated hers, riding her hard like she craved. She shook underneath him and squeezed down around him. She took a quick breath only to spend it screaming his name.

He coaxed a long climax out of her before submitting to his own, calling her name, too.

They both finished and he rolled onto his back, dragging her with him. "Claire, you turn me into an animal."

"You do it to me, too, Luc. Me, too." She was becoming someone stronger and tougher, but she wasn't sure if she was strong or tough enough to deal with their inevitable separation.

10

"I WISH WE HAD SOME marshmallows." Claire snuggled against Luc as they sat next to the fire later that night.

"I can get some grubs if you want to cook something white and squishy on a stick," he offered, only grunting slightly when she elbowed him.

"Ugh. That is so gross."

"Take the plunge. You know you'll have to eat them sooner or later. May as well get it over now where you won't embarrass yourself."

She made a face at him.

"Eh, you'll be happy to eat them if need be. I was, once. All part of surviving in the jungle."

"Would you ever return to San Lucas?"

"San Lucas." He wrinkled his face. "Not my first choice. But I would if it were my duty, and only then. And primarily my duty would be to my teammates to make sure they didn't get killed."

Claire wondered if she was part of his duty, as well. "I do realize it's not all lying around and picking bananas and coconuts off the tree. My mother did mention some rough times, like when they all caught some intestinal parasite and were, um, sick to their stomachs for several days."

Luc didn't seem impressed. "Whoopee. If you haven't gotten some stomach bug, you haven't lived in the jungle."

"And she said two tribes didn't get along and her father had to patch up several men."

He rolled his eyes. "You ever think your mother might have cleaned up her stories for your benefit? You being a kid an' all. You learned about the nice parts of their lives—like those prairie pioneer girl books my sisters read when we were young. Only for your mother it was 'Little House in the Jungle'."

Claire smiled. She had loved those pioneer girl books—still had her original copies from childhood.

He continued, "She probably didn't want to tell you about the disease, the violence, the unpretty parts of it. That was the *only* part I saw."

"Why do you hate San Lucas so much? You get a funny look on your face whenever we talk about it."

He shook his head. "Claire, *cher,* I've been in the army long enough to go to some real shitholes, but San Lucas is the worst of the worst."

"But why?" she persisted. "Surely lots of those other places had warring tribes, parasites and dangerous animals. Why does San Lucas bother you?"

"Your father ever tell you why they chose me to train you? Over all the experienced jungle survival instructors and experts in the whole U.S. Army, why did they pick me?"

She shrugged. "They said you traveled there for several weeks and you knew the country well."

He snorted. "Too damn well. Look, I can't tell you why my team and I were there, but we were deep inside the borders, cruising in a small boat down the Río de la Selva—"

"Near the settlement?" she asked eagerly.

"South." He fingered the hilt of his machete, which was lying in its sheath on the ground next to him. "We came under attack. An RPG was fired into the boat."

"RPG?"

"Rocket-propelled grenade," he explained. "Low-tech but makes a hell of an explosion."

"Oh, my gosh. Were you hurt?" He had so many different scars she couldn't tell which were which.

"Some. Olie and I were farthest away from the impact, so we got dumped into the water. He made it to the other riverbank but I got swept downstream."

"Was it just you two? What happened to the rest of the team?"

His face froze. "More guerillas jumped out and emptied their AK-47s into the river. Missed some of the team who were already cut up by shrapnel, a couple others got shot in the shoulders or legs, and T-Bone, well, they got him."

"Got him?" She tightened her fingers around his.

"Right in the chest." He thumped his own. "I saw him get hit. He sank like a stone—nothing I could do."

"Oh, Luc, that's terrible." She had held her mother while she died, but her death was grindingly inevitable, a relief after weeks of suffering.

"I swam hard, but the blast stunned me and it was all I could do to keep from drowning. It was high-water season and the rapids took me away. Wound up going downstream in the wrong fork—through a long, deep gorge where I couldn't get out of the water."

"How far did you go in the river?"

"Afterward, we figured it was about twenty miles as the crow flies. As the Green Beret walks, it was a bit more."

"And you walked all the way back?"

"I couldn't go back, exactly. That's where they shot at us, after all." His dry tone didn't quite disguise his anger at what had happened. "I had to track back to the fork and down the correct branch to the local military installation that had been our rendezvous point."

"How far was it anyway?"

"A hundred miles. I was trekking for three weeks."

Her mouth fell open. "All that way by yourself? Without anyone else?"

He started to speak and hesitated.

"Did you have any company on your way? A local tribe or something?"

He sighed. "I did have company for a few days. Her name was Angélique."

"Figures you'd find a woman even in the jungle," she muttered.

His laugh was short. "Angélique was a baby."

"A baby?" She sat upright and stared down into his face, even though she couldn't see him well in the dark. "What in the world was a baby doing in the jungle?"

"Her family left her there."

11

Luc knew Claire had no idea what he was talking about. Guess her mother had never filled her in on the less-savory local customs. "She probably hadn't ever been named, but I called her Angélique. She was a newborn with a bilateral cleft lip and cleft palate, as well, as far as I could tell. We didn't cover a whole lot of pediatrics in my medical training."

"That's where the lip doesn't grow together before birth, right? And a hole in the roof of the mouth?"

"Right."

"But I saw a commercial on TV for a charity that helps fix babies like that." Her smooth brow furrowed in confusion. "Why didn't her family bring her to the mission? Dr. Schmidt would have made arrangements for her to be treated."

Luc shook his head. "I don't know. She was all alone when I found her. I even thought that maybe because of her condition she'd been left to die. Some tribes believe disabled children are unfit to live."

She gasped. "And you took her with you." She knew him well.

"What else could I do?" He'd woven a sling of vines and leaves to carry the black-haired girl against his chest. She had stared at him with dark, hazy eyes, amazingly accepting of the total stranger who was carrying her through thick jungle. "I purified water for her and crushed some berries, but…" He shrugged helplessly. He'd even boiled some snake meat, but snake broth and berry juice were no food for a newborn.

"And she died." Claire's voice was full of sorrow.

"Oui." His throat caught. "She had newborn jaundice—comes from not having enough mother's milk. In her case, not any. She got more and more yellow until, well…" He was horrified to hear a sob tear loose. From him. What the hell? Green Berets weren't supposed to cry.

Claire gathered him into her arms, rocking him as if he were the baby. She kissed his forehead and hugged him. "You did your best, Luc. No wonder you hate San Lucas de la Selva—you saw the absolute worst of it."

He sat up and hastily wiped his cheeks, grateful for the dim light. "Life is cheap there. Maybe a tribe could have kept that baby alive long enough to get her to the mission or the military base, but luck was not on her side. *C'est tout.* That's all."

CLAIRE AWOKE SUDDENLY from a messy, disturbing dream where she was lost in a green maze. No surprise where that one had come from. Luc was still asleep, his breathing deep and even. He'd tried to hide his emotions, but she had felt the tears on his face and heard the heartbreak in his voice. Of all the reasons he hated and mistrusted the jungle, she never would have guessed his sad story of baby Angélique. She sniffled back tears, as well.

What good had anyone done for the people of San Lucas if such a thing were still possible? Common, even, to echo Luc's statement. Where, or how, could respect for an ancient culture supercede an innocent life?

She rolled to her side, empathizing with her mother, who must have run into similar disturbing situations. Naively, Claire thought people would come to the mission in a situation like that. After fifty years of co-existence, the tribes surely knew the mission offered medical care.

She also grudgingly admitted to herself that she owed her father an apology. He had tried to talk to her about the realities of life and death in the Amazon, but she had thought he exaggerated in order to discourage her.

But Luc's experience was a cold wake-up. If she went, she would need that same wake-up. If? She bit her lip. Was she chickening out? Fear of leaving her comfy existence, or the realization that being with Luc was becoming more and more important every hour they spent together?

It seemed impossible they had only know each other for a week. She'd dated her couple previous boyfriends for months and never felt this way about any of them. Of course, few men could measure up to Luc.

She let her mind wander to what might happen if she did cancel her plans. Would Luc even want to further their relationship? He'd never indicated that their rustic interlude was anything more than temporary. They hadn't even exchanged phone number or e-mail addresses.

His sleepy drawl surprised her. "I can practically hear the wheels turnin' in your head." He rolled to his side and draped his arm over her. "Sorry I told you that sad tale—ain't never told no one but Olie and my team. Don't you worry about it."

But she did worry. She closed her eyes as he unexpectedly kissed the top of her head. *"Fais do-do, cher."*

Claire's lips pulled into a small smile. Maybe she would *"fais do-do,"* or "go nighty-night." If there was one thing Luc's training had taught her, it was to sleep when she could.

CLAIRE MAY AS WELL have stayed awake all night for all the good it did her. Luc had hiked her for miles and miles the next day. Despite her special socks and padding, her feet had broken open again and she wouldn't have been surprised to see blood oozing out of her boots. She staggered into their camp behind Luc. She supposed he might have stopped if he'd heard her collapse, but then again, maybe not. He had woken silent and pulled into himself again, obviously regretting he'd ever mentioned his hideous jungle journey.

She almost regretted it, too. Of all the things he could have opened up to her about—his childhood, his family, his training…but no. He had to break open his heart and show her the absolute rawest thing anyone ever experienced.

It broke her heart, too. All day, she'd had nothing but time to think about cheap life and easy death in the Amazon. What a fool she had been to think she could do anything. She wasn't even strong enough to listen to his story, much less live it.

She dropped her gear next to the tent. It could shatter for all she cared.

"Drink some water, Claire."

She ignored Luc. What did he care if she drank water or not? He was the one trying to run her into the ground. She crawled onto the bedding, not bothering to check it for bugs or animals.

"Get up." He stood over her, his arms crossed his chest.

"Buzz off." Why wasn't he even sweating?

"Get up, Claire." His black brows drew into a deep vee.

"No, Luc, this is too hard."

"What?" His eyebrows slammed together.

"I've had enough."

"Enough what?"

"Enough training. I'll never need to do any of this. I promise I'll never go off on my own. I'll always have somebody around to help me." She flopped onto her back and rested her forearm across her eyes. She squeaked as he tossed her over his shoulder. "Hey, put me down!"

"You ever gon' take a boat ride in San Lucas? Take a plane ride? Boats sink and planes crash. Then what you gon' do?" He stalked toward the watering hole.

Oh, no, he wouldn't. He did. "Luc!" Her scream was cut off as she hit the cold spring water and sank.

She sputtered to the surface. "You bully! You creep! You—you bastard!"

He squatted at the bank, unimpressed with her insults. "Who are you, Claire Cook? You some put-upon Southern Belle on your faintin' couch? You some Blanche Dubois? Well, this ain't no cheap dinner theatre production of *A Streetcar Named Desire*. This is goddamn real life and death here."

"Luc!" She wiped water out of her face, treading water in her boots.

He made no attempt to help her, his jaw tight and black eyes cold. "I've told you this before but it's not sinking in—you cannot depend on strangers. You cannot depend on anyone but yourself. Not me, not yo' papa, not some native dude wandering by who needs a new girlfriend. There is no such thing as the kindness of strangers in the jungle. You save yourself, or you die."

"Why are you being so mean? I tried to learn everything you taught me." She hauled herself out of the spring and sat on a log, water running off her in streams. She hoped it disguised the tears starting to run down her face.

Luc stood, looming over her. "Nobody can teach you mental toughness. You have to learn that for yourself. You have to dig deep, not think or hope, but know that you can survive. The jungle either accepts you or spits you out. It spits out the weak-minded ones."

She glared at him. "I am strong-minded! I'm leaving the country, I'm even leaving the continent. Would a weak-minded person do that?"

"You're going to your mother's hometown. Running to everyone who knew her and will take care of you to honor her memory. Not much of a gamble, is it?"

"Shut up!" Claire leaped to her feet. "At least I'm doing something, learning new things, risking myself. What do you do? You have your job and your teammates, and that's it. I bet they have somebody to go home to at night, but not you. Nobody to care for you, nobody you have to care about. I bet the last person you cared for was that poor little baby, wasn't it?"

Throughout her tirade he had kept a blank expression except for a minute flinch at her last question. "That's right, Claire. I am a weak, damaged man who can't let anyone into his life. Now can we finish your training, or do you want to die in the jungle?"

She stared at him. It was impossible to dent his iron will. Well, it was about time she grew an iron will of her own. "I will not die in the jungle. I will learn all you can teach me, and I will go out and live a true life instead of chasing after death." With that parting shot, she turned her back to him and walked into the woods.

LUC WINCED AS CLAIRE limped away. He'd heard her struggling through the last part of their march, but she needed to be able to walk at least fifteen kilometers without stopping. He'd go to her when she calmed down and examine her poor feet.

He sighed. Maybe he needed to examine himself, as well, remembering her words. Did he really chase after death?

He sat down at the water's edge and stared into its green depths. Yes, he did. He brought death to the enemies of the United States of America, thereby bringing life to the regular soldiers and civilians who would not become their victims. It was a difficult balance, especially considering his extensive medical training—to shoot with one hand and heal with the other.

But the only deaths he regretted were baby Angélique and T-Bone. During T-Bone's memorial service, the unit chaplain had quoted Psalm 121, the soldier's Psalm. "'The sun shall not smite thee by day, nor the moon by night,'" he murmured.

He opened his canteen and splashed some water on his face. It was still his job to make sure nothing smote Claire.

LATER THAT NIGHT, he slipped into the tent and lay down when he was sure she would be asleep. She wasn't. "Luc?" she murmured sleepily.

"Oui."

She rolled over and put her arm over him. "Sorry I said all that awful stuff today."

"S'okay, *cher.*" He tucked her hand into his and kissed her fingers. "I wasn't real kind, either."

"Can't even imagine that. First your friend, then a baby. My mother died peacefully in my arms—that was a blessing at the end." She yawned. "After the funeral was the first time in months we'd been able to take a breath. And of course we felt guilty about that."

Luc blinked. T-Bone had died in his arms, too, but not peacefully. By the time Luc struggled back to so-called civilization, he'd needed several weeks to recover from various parasitic and bacterial infections and regain his weight and strength. Then he'd rejoined his team. Had he ever been able to take a breath? No, but he'd sure felt the guilt.

"Did your friend leave a family behind?"

"Yeah. A wife and three little kids."

Claire was silent for so long he thought she'd fallen asleep. "Love is a risk no matter who you love."

"Your mama must have been a real special lady to have raised you so well."

"Thank you, Luc." She kissed his shoulder. "You would have liked her. She would have understood what you went through in the jungle."

"*Cher,* I don't even understand what I went through in the jungle." It was the first time he'd admitted that to anyone, even himself.

She rested her cheek on his shoulder blade. "Tell me, sweetheart."

He didn't know if it was her calm, sweet voice or the fact she'd called him "sweetheart," but something broke inside him. "Being in Special Forces, you train to be part of your A-team, part of your group, part of something bigger. You always ask yourself what you can do to help the team. When we were attacked, the worst thing was that I wound up alone. I'm not used to that with six sisters." He tried to joke.

"Yes, I know."

"And the baby was company, but then she wasn't." He didn't trust himself to say anything more. "So I was alone again. We talk about it, you know. What it would be like to be taken captive, put in isolation. I was free to move, free to find food and water, but I started to wonder if I'd ever get out."

"What did you do about that?"

He grimaced, glad she couldn't see his face. "I

talked to myself the whole damn time. Carried on long conversations with myself. Not out loud, in my head."

"So you hate being alone but you don't want anyone close to you, either."

"Sounds almost as crazy as my talking to myself, doesn't it?"

"I talk to myself all the time. 'What should I do today? What should I wear?' Heck, I even pretend my mom is there sometimes and I ask her what I should do."

"Nothing wrong with that." Her breath was warm and soft on his cheek, just like the woman herself. He was a man who faced problems head on, but he couldn't face the idea of leaving her.

"I get lonely, too, Luc. Even when I'm around hundreds of people at a party or at the mall, I look at everybody and wonder how I can be so alone. But with you, Luc, I never feel alone," she whispered. "Even if you're off in the woods doing whatever you need to do, I know you're there for me, and all I have to do is call your name."

Luc swallowed hard. "I know what you mean, Claire." It was as close as he could get to admitting how she affected him. "It is kind of nice coming back to camp and having you kiss me hello."

"Would that be so terrible to have when you finished your assignments? Having someone meet your plane and kiss you hello?"

It didn't sound terrible, it sounded wonderful. But

only if it was Claire. Disembarking and seeing her beautiful face light up as she spotted him, laughing out loud as they ran toward each other and kissing as if they could never stop. Then speeding home to jump into bed, not coming up for air for days. It was a deeper and more secret fantasy than any sexual ones he dared admit. "Some of the guys have that." They had sweet chubby babies and kids who waved American flags and screamed when they spotted their papas.

"But not you."

The image of black-haired, brown-eyed *bébés* in Claire's arms popped like a soap bubble. "No, Claire, not me." Silence grew between them, not the comfortable silence they enjoyed together. "If it makes any difference, I've never had that. If I ever could, it would be with you."

Hot tears leaked into his T-shirt. Oh, no, she was crying. He rolled over and scooped her into his arms. "Don't cry, Claire. I'm a bastard who doesn't deserve even one drop of your tears."

"Oh, Luc, don't say that. You're good, honest, decent. A real hero for people to look up to."

His hand froze as he stroked her hair. A hero for people to look up to? He had just swept this girl away from her well-meaning father, brought her out to the woods to push her through harsh conditions, and now she was talking about him as if he were some kind of hero? He'd been accused of arrogance before, but this took the cake.

His own throat clogged and he could only press her face against him as she sobbed. What the hell was wrong with him? Thank God he was taking her back tomorrow before he wrecked her even more.

She quieted after several minutes, worn out from her emotional and physical exhaustion.

"Go to sleep, Claire." He kissed the top of her sweet-smelling head.

She gave a shuddering sigh. "Okay, Luc." She yawned. "Love you."

His eyes flew wide in shock as she subsided into sleep. Love? Love? She didn't say that…she couldn't believe that—it was impossible. She didn't really know him. He was a beat-up, worn-out soldier who didn't deserve a woman like her.

He'd deliver her back to her father, back to her quiet, peaceful life. Back to the life where she could forget Luc Boudreaux and find a man who was worthy of the jewel that was Claire Cook.

12

CLAIRE'S STOMACH HAD been in knots the whole drive to Ft. Bragg. She was awake for the trip this time and got to see the South Carolina Low Country scenery before turning into the piney woods of North Carolina. It was pretty but not enough to take her mind off their upcoming arrival in civilization.

He stopped at the gates leading into Ft. Bragg and showed his military ID. They drove through the base for several minutes before reaching the Special Forces installation. The guards greeted Luc by name and waved them through. He pulled over in the parking lot next to the headquarters and jumped out of the truck without saying anything to her.

Claire sat for a second. That wasn't a good sign. She didn't expect a giant make-out session in the parking lot but she thought he'd at least say something to her.

She jumped down from the truck and circled to the tailgate, where he was unlocking her gear. "So, here we are."

"Yeah."

"Need some help with the luggage?"

A glimmer of humor peeked out. "No, I think I can manage. Ready to go see your father?"

She pursed her lips. Her daddy was sure to have plenty to say about her disappearing for a week, but she had plenty to say about her "spy in the sky" supplies. "He'll be pleased with how much I've learned." She winked at Luc, hoping he'd smile back.

He didn't, hefting her duffel bag. Maybe he was unsure of what to say, but she'd been thinking. "Luc, I was thinking about that girl in the trailer out in the middle of nowhere."

"Yeah?"

"What if I stayed here and took a job working with families like that…" She trailed off at the look of alarm on his face.

"Stay here, where? The U.S. or Fayetteville? Give up your plans for San Lucas?"

Stung, she snapped, "I'd thought you'd be happy. You're always telling me what a hellhole it is."

"That part hasn't changed. But I think you got tough enough to manage for the kind of work you'd be doing. And your *maman*'s friends will look after you."

"I can look after myself now. But I thought after what we—that time we spent together…" His face turned blank and hard, and she hated how her voice trailed away. He looked as if he were about to undergo a particularly unpleasant mission. Maybe breaking up with her was. "Oh. I see." She lifted her chin.

"Good luck, Claire." He cupped her jaw and

brushed a thumb across her cheek. Then he walked away.

"Kiss my ass, Luc!" she shouted after him. He wanted to be the Noble Soldier and walk off into the sunset, confident he was doing her a favor by leaving her first.

"What?" He turned back in shock.

"You heard me. You're running away."

His jaw clenched. "You should know, Claire. You're running off to the jungle because you can't stand up to your father if you stay in Virginia."

"I offered to stay with *you* since I love you, you dope."

The *L* word fell between them like an unexploded grenade. "I never asked you to love me."

This wasn't going at all how she'd planned. "Then you shouldn't have been so wonderful."

He looked like he sucked on a lemon. "You got the wrong man, Claire. You want wonderful, you keep looking. I'm not. I'm broken, no good for you, *cher.*"

She shook her head. "I would rather spend a minute with you than a lifetime with another man."

"You don't have that choice—sacrificing yourself for me."

He still didn't understand that he was worth any sacrifice. "I don't have that choice since you're taking it away. You and my father have more in common than you think—you both know what's best for me. At least he does it out of love for me. You're only doing it to protect yourself."

"I'm trying to protect you, Claire."

"Well, don't. I don't want your protection. I have developed your fabled mental toughness. I love you enough to let you go." Tears stung her eyes and she knew she had to get away before he saw them. "Goodbye, Luc." This time, she was the one to turn her back on him and walk away.

And he didn't stop her.

AFTER HER FATHER HAD finished hugging her and lecturing her, after Janey had stopped giving her surreptitious stares of concern, after settling herself in her original hotel room with the clean, soft, empty bed, Claire locked herself in the bathroom and turned on the fan. The face that stared back was different. Tanned, more freckled, and thinner, but another less-definable change shadowed her eyes and hollowed her cheeks. Was it heartbreak?

It had to be, since her image suddenly blurred and crumbled, her tears running down the drain—just like her dreams of a life with Luc.

"WELL, LOOK WHAT THE cat dragged in—can it be? Why, it's my long-lost sergeant." Olie folded his arms across his chest and glared at Luc. "We thought a gator'd finally gotten you."

"Sergeant First Class Luc Boudreaux, reporting for duty." Luc snapped him a salute.

Olie pursed his lips. "You're lucky you're not reporting for a court martial, boy. Or a public flogging in the town square, if the good congressman had his druthers. Oh, at ease." He shook his head in annoyance.

Luc dropped into Olie's visitor chair.

"What do you have to say for yourself, Rage?"

Luc shook himself a bit. It had been a week since anyone had called him that, and the funny thing was, the rage he'd been carrying around since T-Bone and Angélique died had lifted. "I trained Miss Cook in basic survival skills as best as I could, considering the differences in terrain and climate compared to San Lucas. She is now somewhat proficient in food-gathering, fire-starting and map-reading. We even conducted a mini-SERE exercise." He forced himself not to think of how he had captured her and she had shown him who was really in charge.

Olie's eyes narrowed. Some of Luc's memories must have shown up on his face. "Is that all you trained her in, Sergeant? Because I distinctly recalling you giving me your word as a soldier and gentleman that Miss Cook was safe in your company. That you would not lay a single finger on her pretty self."

Luc couldn't meet Olie's glare. He had sworn, and he had broken his word.

"Dammit all, Rage." Olie thunked his fist down on the desk. "I specifically warned you she was too pretty and you were too horny to take her out in the woods alone, but do you listen to me? No, you don't."

"It wasn't like that," he growled.

"It wasn't?" Olie drummed his fingers. "I get it now—it was her idea, right? Maybe she's one of those party girls who wanted to get laid by a real American fighting man before leaving the country. I can understand that—you were horny, she was slutty—"

Luc was on his feet grabbing Olie by the lapels and giving him a good shake. "Don't you ever talk about Claire like that!"

Olie stared coolly at him. "So that's how it is."

Luc shoved him into his seat and spun away, shaking. He'd never lost his cool like that, much less laid hands on a superior officer. Olie could have him up on charges and Luc would deserve every one of them.

"Luc. Sit." Olie's tone was gentle.

Luc rubbed his face in an effort to regain his composure before turning around. "What do you mean, 'So that's how it is'?"

"You ever been in love before?"

"What?" Luc's eyes bugged out. "Hell no, and I ain't in love now."

"You say so." Olie steepled his fingers together, scrutinizing him head to toe. Luc hated that gesture.

"Yeah, I do say so. We did get, um, close, but I was upfront with her about how it never worked out with me getting close to one particular woman."

"You mean, fall in love?" Olie asked dryly.

He shrugged, not even wanting to say the word. "Claire tried to tell me it was okay if I ever had to leave, that she would be waiting for me when I came back."

"She was willing to give up her dream of doing good in the jungle to hang around Fayetteville, North Carolina, in that dingy bachelor pad of yours? Willing to stay here for the chance of being with you when you came home from your deployment? Away from her friends, her family, her job?"

Luc shifted. "We never discussed any details. I told her she'd always have regrets if she didn't follow her dreams. So…" He raised his palms. "I guess she's gonna follow them."

Throughout his explanation, Olie's ruddy face grew darker and darker until he looked like a tomato with blond eyebrows. It had been a long time since Luc had seen him that angry. "What? You think I should go along with this? It'll bring her nothing but heartache. You, of all people, should know that."

"We're not talking about me, you stupid jackass! You utter and complete moron." Olie called him another couple of profane names. "You dare call yourself a Green Beret? Wah, wah, wah." Olie leaped to his feet and came around his desk. "'I found this girl who loves my ugly ass and I don't have the balls to do anything about it.' You make me sick, Rage."

"Hey!" Luc jumped up, too, going toe-to-toe with his CO.

"Chickenshit." Olie shoved him in the chest. "Life

is handing you a gift and you're throwing it down and stomping your boots all over it."

"A gift?" Luc clenched his fists. "You think Claire will call it a gift when I go overseas for months or years at a time? When I don't come home for Christmas? Or if I *do* come home in a box and they hand her a folded flag? More like a mistake."

Olie stabbed his finger at T-Bone's photo on the wall. "Go ask Mariel," Olie thundered. Mariel was T-Bone's widow. "Go ask their kids. Was marrying him a mistake? Were their three kids a mistake?"

"No, of course not," he muttered.

"I know you went to visit Mariel once you got patched up. What did she tell you?"

Luc swallowed hard.

"Come on, what did she say?"

"She thanked me for trying to save him. That it wasn't my fault Tom died."

"Damn right. It was the fault of that SOB who sent an RPG into our boat and shot us up. What else?"

Luc wiped his stinging eyes. "She said she would have rather spent five minutes with Tom than fifty years with another man. But…" He stopped in shock. Claire had told him the same thing, almost word for word.

"And she meant it." Olie wiped his own eyes. "What woman is willing to put up with that? What woman would cry for us if we died, Rage? Only a woman who truly loves her Green Beret, that's who."

"Claire would." He looked at Olie, his heart pounding. "She said she loved me enough to let me go."

Olie crashed his palm down on the table. "Well, hallelujah, you're not as dumb as you look."

"But I let her go."

"I take that back—you're even dumber."

LUC OPENED THE FRONT DOOR to his apartment and tossed the fistful of mail onto his coffee table. His place wasn't much, but it was better than living on base. It was even clean for now, since his buddy's wife ran a cleaning company and had gone through the one bedroom, bath, kitchen and living room with her mop and vacuum since he'd returned from the sandbox.

At least here he could have some privacy, which had been seriously in short supply while he and his team were out in the field. Here he could sit and drink a beer reclining in his black leather sectional while he watched the huge flat-screen TV.

He pulled out a beer and flipped up the recliner while he surfed through the channels. Local news, nothing good on sports, some weepy chick flick, national news with talking heads yapping about Afghanistan and Iraq as if they could even find the places on a map. As if they could even find their asses with two hands and a map. He told them all where to go using several rude French verbs and was about to turn off the TV when Claire's father, of all people, popped up on C-SPAN. The man looked good on TV, Luc had to admit, a wise elder statesman-type. Luc shook his head. Bad enough he had to get that woman out of his system without seeing reminders of her on TV.

He shut off the TV and rubbed his eyes. Maybe he should try to get some sleep. He was planning to leave for Louisiana in a couple days and wouldn't get much rest sleeping on his parents' couch.

No more tents or swamps, at least not for now. Tonight Luc would sleep on a bed for the first time in a week.

Sleep alone for the first time since he and Claire had started making love.

And love was what it was.

He loved Claire. He should have known that back in the woods, should have known that when he'd dropped her off to her father, when he'd shoved her out of his life.

What was he supposed to do now? He stared blankly at the dark TV screen, as blank as his mind except for the overwhelming loss. For a man who made life-and-death decisions on a frequent basis, he was sure screwing up. He had used up more of his lives than a cat, and chances were he might not live to be an old man. Claire was only twenty-four. T-Bone's widow was only a couple years older.

He sighed and set down his beer. It was making him too sentimental, anyway. He reached for his mail, automatically flipping aside the junk into one pile, bills into another. There was no personal mail. Never was.

Finally, the catalogs on the bottom. He shook his head. What the hell kind of mailing list had he gotten on? Sure, he understood the knife and gun catalogs, but home decoration and fluffy gift catalogs? He was about to toss one aside when the model on the cover caught his eye.

No, it wasn't Claire, although her peachy skin and dark hair was a close match. Calling himself ten thousand kinds of a fool, he opened the pages to look for any more pictures of the model. He didn't have any photos of Claire.

After several pages of clever T-shirts, puppy statues and hand-painted wineglasses, he was about ready to close it when he spotted a ring. A simple gold band, it was engraved with the French script *"Vous et nul autre."* You, and no other.

Luc felt like the time Olie had sucker-punched him in the gut during hand-to-hand combat training. He read the catalog description—a reproduction of a medieval ring given by one lover to another.

You, and no other. That was who Claire was. Only Claire—no other woman would ever do for him. He flipped the recliner lever and leaped up. He knew what he had to do, and it didn't look like he'd sleep in a bed tonight, either.

"Here. Blow." Janey stuffed yet another tissue into Claire's hand. She'd been crying so much, it was hard to see the box. She wiped her eyes and her nose, but the tears didn't stop.

"Claire, you've been crying for three hours straight. If you don't stop, I'm gonna slip a sleeping pill into your milk shake to knock you out."

Her eyes widened. "You wouldn't."

Janey gave her a baleful glance. "Try me. You're making yourself sick with weeping over this guy? And you've only known him a week."

She dabbed her nose. "I told Luc I loved him. He was the first man I ever said that to, did you know that?"

Janey nodded.

"I told him I loved him and he said, 'Oh.'"

"'Oh'?" Janey's face mirrored Claire's own dismay. "Oh. Anything else?"

"He said he couldn't love me. He said he knew we'd become close over the past week or so, but he didn't want it to interfere with my plans. In other words, don't let the tent flap hit you on the way out." She sniffled again. "It only took that bastard one week to make me fall in love with him, and he told me to go ahead with my plans."

"You should go ahead with your plans. You know he will."

"That's right, he will. And to think I was thinking about canceling my trip to San Lucas to be with him."

"Geez, Claire, did you tell him that?" Janey grimaced.

"Well, not just to be with him. I thought I could call the social services office near Norfolk to see if they had any assignments nearby."

"Nearby to home, or nearby to Fayetteville?"

She shrugged. "I did mention Fayetteville."

Janey shook her head. "No wonder he bailed on you. You probably turned his life upside down, too."

"Oh, I did not. He probably does this all the time. Takes a woman out into the woods, trains her in survival skills, makes her fall in love with him, dumps her back in civilization literally and figuratively..." She balled up her tissue and threw it away, like Luc had thrown her away.

"Sounds like a lot of work for a guy who's hot enough to go into a bar and get a dozen invitations for sex within the first ten minutes."

Claire needed to stop thinking about Luc having sex with other women or else she was going to cry again. "Speaking of sexy guys in bars, whatever happened between you and that blond guy Olie?"

Janey's face hardened. "Never you mind that. Let's just say he's off my Christmas card list." She tapped her fingers on the table. "So Luc said he didn't love you?"

"No, he said he couldn't love me. Big difference, huh?"

"Actually, yes. Maybe he does love you, but he thinks it's impossible."

"He's worried about impossible?" Claire jumped to her feet and paced like a madwoman. "Janey, this guy has done more impossible things in his life than a million other guys. He survived being exploded out of a boat, shot at and nearly drowned before trekking one hundred miles alone through some of the worst jungle in the world and—let's face it—he trained me to not get lost in the woods and to skin and gut small animals without throwing up. If he can do that, he can practically leap tall buildings with a single bound."

"Luc's a real hero, Claire. Olie said he's being awarded for a Silver Star for the enemy reconnaissance he conducted in Afghanistan. That's classified, though."

"Well, he's not earning any medals for valor from me. He's a chicken when it comes to important stuff like love and happiness."

"You can't make him into somebody he's not, and you can't be someone you're not. If he wants to love you, that has to come from within him. Remember Felicia?"

"From college?"

"The very one. She picked out a boyfriend who liked blondes, so she went blond. He liked tall girls, so she wore heels all the time and wound up needing the foot doctor. He liked dumb girls so she flunked most of her classes. And what happened to her after the university asked her to leave for bad grades?"

Claire winced at the memory. "Her boyfriend dumped her for a short, brunette Rhodes scholar. He said his new girlfriend was 'genuine.' And Felicia got arrested for breaking all the windows in his car."

"Bad hair, bad feet, bad grades and a criminal record. The moral of this story is to be yourself. What do you want to do? Not what do you want to do if Luc does this, or if Luc does that. What does Claire Adeline Cook want for herself?"

"I don't know. I'm a chicken."

"Don't tell me that! You were the one who bathed and fed her mother as she was dying. You were the one who took care of her dad when he was so sad he wanted to die. You dummy, you've been brave all along. Eating snakes and sleeping in trees has nothing to do with bravery."

Claire stopped midstep. "You know what, Janey? You're right. I've had mental toughness the whole time, and Luc hasn't. Just because he's a hard-ass soldier doesn't mean he knows doodley-squat about anything—especially this love stuff. He was all gung-ho when we were having sex four or five times a day, but he started kissing my hair and telling me things he'd never told anyone else before. It was too much for him to manage."

"Sex four or five times a day?" Janey whispered faintly. She blinked several times and fanned herself.

"Yes, and it was great," she said. "He showed me things I never even dreamed of doing."

Janey hesitated briefly and gave in to her curiosity. "Like what?"

Luc didn't love her, so why would he care if she bragged a bit? Claire smugly gave her the general outline, enjoying being the sexpert for once. But when she described how they'd acted out several fantasies, Janey interrupted her with a groan.

"Enough, enough! A week ago you were practically a virgin. Now you're into roleplaying?"

"When the right man comes along, Janey my girl, anything is possible."

"Keep it up and you'll make me sorry Olie and I didn't hook up that night."

"I expect you to tell me what happened with that."

"Not now. One crisis is enough. Focus, Claire. Get your mind off Luc's poor overworked ding-dong and figure out what you want to do about the rest of him."

"Nothing." She shook her head. "He knows where I am. He can come to me."

"What if he doesn't?"

Claire sighed. "I leave for Virginia tomorrow, and I leave for San Lucas three days after that. If I don't see him before then, I'll know he wasn't brave enough to fight for me, decorated hero or no."

"CLAIRE, HONEY? CAN I come in?" Her dad stood in her bedroom doorway at home in Virginia.

She looked up from where she was sitting on the window seat in her old comfy robe and pajamas. "I thought you were asleep, Dad." She'd found it impossible to sleep, as well, and had been staring out the darkened window, trying not to think of Luc. He hadn't called her hotel in Fayetteville, hadn't called her house in Virginia. She guessed she knew his answer.

"No, I had some paperwork to read and well…" He shoved a hand through his silver hair. "I don't want you flying off to San Lucas before we have a chance to talk."

"Talk about what?"

"Anything you want, Claire. Your trip, your time in the woods, your…" He trailed off again.

"My mother?" she guessed.

"Her, too." He sat facing her on the seat.

She didn't want to talk about her mother, so she picked option one. "I leave the day after tomorrow, and I'm really excited." But she sounded about as excited as someone looking forward to cutting the grass.

"I'm glad." Dad looked away. "I'm sorry about how I handled everything, including those stupid electronic trackers. I shouldn't have tried to talk you out of going to San Lucas and I shouldn't have pressured you into last-minute survival training." He finally smiled at her. "You finally ran away from home—most kids do that when they're teenagers."

"I guess I'm a late bloomer."

"Dads never like to see their daughters grow up into beautiful women, but…" He lifted his hands in a helpless gesture. "You've become a beautiful woman and I'm very proud of you."

Claire stared at him. "Really?"

"Of course. Don't I always introduce you as 'my beautiful, talented daughter, Claire'?"

"Oh, that." She leaned against the wall. "At political rallies? I could look like a plow horse in a skirt and everyone would still clap."

Dad frowned. "Just because I'm a politician doesn't make me a liar about you. My constituents can see for themselves, you know. And if you want to use your talents to help those unfortunate souls in San Lucas, you have my blessing and support." He rested his loafer on his opposite knee. "Hmm. I may need to organize a congressional fact-finding mission to San Lucas. After you get settled in, of course," he added hastily as she narrowed her eyes at him.

"I will be fine. I actually did learn a lot about jungle survival from Luc—Sergeant First Class Boudreaux."

"Did you?" Dad tapped a finger on his ankle.

She took a deep breath, surprised at the pain that hit her middle when she thought of Luc. "Yes, how to find clean water and food, map-reading, avoiding poisonous snakes—did I tell you how I swung myself into a tree branch with an angry cottonmouth swimming at me?"

"Yes." He closed his eyes and shuddered. "I'd prefer to forget that horrible image. But you did well. I knew Sergeant Boudreaux was the right man for the job."

Claire tried to keep a neutral expression on her face, glad for the dark room.

"Of course, I never expected you to disappear into the rural Low Country alone with the man," her dad mused. "If I'd known that, I would have picked someone who wasn't quite so handsome and dashing."

"Don't forget heroic." She couldn't keep a tinge of bitterness from her voice. "Janey says he's up for a Silver Star for action in Afghanistan." Too bad he was a coward when it came to her.

"Indeed." He nodded. "I hope he enjoys the medal because if he's hurt you, they'll present it to him along with his discharge papers."

"What?"

"I may be an old widowed dad, but I can still recognize certain manly emotions, shall we say. And that young Cajun had a boatload of them crossing his face when you left."

"Like what?"

"Regret, sorrow, affection…maybe even love?" He lifted a bushy eyebrow.

She was already shaking her head. "No, Dad. Luc may have been fond of me after working together so closely, but his love is for the army and his band of brothers. That's how he thinks of his team. No women allowed." She gave him a weak smile.

Dad grunted, obviously not convinced. "If you won't let me abuse my congressional powers and ruin his military career, can I at least punch him in the nose?"

That shocked a giggle out of her. Punching seemed so low-class for a man like her patrician father. "We're Virginians, Dad. How about you horsewhip him?" They had several whips in the stable.

"Excellent." He brightened immediately and declaimed in a theatrically hammy Southern accent, "'Suh, you have offended the Cook family honuh. Prepay-uh for your trouncin'.'"

She was laughing hard enough to hurt her sides. "Oh, Dad, you should have been a professional actor."

He grinned at her. "My dear, I already am. Some days the Capitol dome is the best-looking theater in America."

"It will be strange to be so far from it," Claire mused.

"Your mother threatened to go back to San Lucas at least once every election cycle. But she loved me more than I deserved and hung around anyway."

"I miss her."

"I do, too." Dad pulled her into a hug. "I wasn't much help when she was so sick, I'm sorry to say. But you were the brave one. You always have been." He kissed her forehead.

She choked back a laugh. "Everybody has been telling me that—that I was brave all along but didn't realize it."

"It's true. You are a wonderful young woman, and woe to anyone who doesn't know it." He wrinkled his nose as if he'd smelled something bad. "Even that doltish young sergeant."

"Dad, forget about him."

"Can't I lie in wait for him outside his barracks late one night and jump him?"

She laughed. Her dad, a silver-haired, Mr. Rogers

look-alike, leaping onto the back of a Special Forces soldier. "No."

"How about I key his monster truck?"

"No."

"Puncture those huge tires?"

"No."

"Sprinkle itching powder into his army-issue boxers?"

Claire decided not to tell her dad Luc wore briefs. "No." She was laughing too hard to speak clearly by then.

"Curses, foiled again." He twisted an imaginary mustache. "Then he'll just have to live with his own regrets like the rest of us."

"Did Mom have any regrets?"

"Only that she couldn't stay with us longer. None about how she lived her life, and especially none about you."

"That's a good way to live."

Her dad kissed her cheek. "Amen."

13

CLAIRE WAS DEEP IN her closet, pulling out the big suitcase she planned to pack medical supplies in for her trip to San Lucas. It was customary to bring a tiny suitcase of clothing and personal items and your approximate body weight in bandages, antibiotics and antimalarial medications.

The doorbell rang and she called downstairs for Louella to answer it. When the bell rang again, she remembered Louella was running errands in Cooksville, so she jogged downstairs in her denim cutoffs and lime-green tank top.

She pulled open the front door. "Yes?" Her voice trailed away. Luc stood on the wide front porch in a button-down black shirt and matching pants. He looked lean, dark and heartbreakingly handsome. "Luc. What are you doing here?"

"I came to see you."

"Oh, come in." Her stomach quivered as he followed her into the high-ceilinged entryway. "Would you like some lemonade? Louella made it fresh this morning with real lemons and mint simple syrup. She loves making everything from scratch," she called over her shoulder as she scurried into the kitchen.

Over the past few days, she'd imagined a hundred different scenarios if Luc actually did show up. He'd drop to his knees to beg her forgiveness; she'd chew him out and point a haughty finger toward the door. But she hadn't imagined she'd run away from him and offer him a cold beverage.

She pulled the pitcher from the fridge before he stopped her. "Claire, I don't want any lemonade."

"You don't?" She stood there stupidly as her hands sweated more than the pitcher.

"No." He took it from her and set it in the fridge. "I've been thinking about what happened between us and I realized it shouldn't have ended that way."

"Oh. So you came to end it another way." Talk about twisting the knife.

He grabbed her clammy hand. "I…" He blew out his breath in a nervous puff. "I don't want it to end at all."

"You don't?" Her fingers tightened on his. "What about all your talk about how you didn't want to have anyone waiting for you because of the danger involved?"

He shook his head. "The only danger is not being with you."

Claire couldn't believe he was saying the things she longed to hear. "Two days ago, you were telling me about all your buddies who got dumped overseas. What if you have regrets the second I fly away? Do I have to dread opening my mail for fear of a 'Dear Jane' letter?"

He caressed her cheek. "Like a very wise and beautiful woman once told me, sometimes a man has to stop chasing death and live a true life. And I want to live that true life with you." He pulled a gray velvet pouch from his pocket and tipped a gold circle into his palm. "Read it."

She picked it up from his warm hand. "*'Vous et nul autre.' 'You and no other.'"* The ancient words of love were engraved in a medieval script on the ring. It was beautiful and she could hardly believe he was offering it to her. "Oh, Luc. Where did you get this?" She pressed her hand against her mouth.

"The operator was a bit worried when I asked where the warehouse was, but when I told her I was a soldier and needed it for my girlfriend, she gave me their address in Atlanta."

"You drove to Atlanta for this?" That was a five-hour drive from Fayetteville and another seven-hour drive to Cooksville.

He nodded, his expression nonchalant but his eyes gleaming. "I drove all night and bought it when they opened at oh-eight-hundred. Then I stopped at home, took a shower and drove here."

Her eyes widened. "When was the last time you slept?" He was probably hallucinating from sleep deprivation by now. She hoped he remembered giving her the ring when he woke up tomorrow.

"A while ago. But that's not important, Claire. You are. We are."

Her eyes filled. "Oh, Luc. I thought you didn't care." His face blurred and he pulled her into his arms.

"Don't cry, *cher* Claire. *Je t'aime toujours, ma douce.*"

She cried even harder. It was the first time he had told her he loved her, would love her forever. "I love you, too, always."

He gave a big sigh of relief. "We love each other, right?" She nodded. "Give me a kiss, then, sweetheart."

She tipped her mouth up to his, her wet cheeks sliding over his as he kissed her gently.

"But I'm leaving for San Lucas the day after tomorrow!" she wailed. "I can't let them down—I have fifty pounds of medication that they're counting on."

"They're counting on more than that, Claire. They're counting on *you.*" He kissed her again. "Go to San Lucas, *cher.* I'll be waiting for you when you come home."

"But what if you get deployed before I return?"

"Then you'll be waiting for me when I come off that plane, waving that American flag and running to kiss me hello. We got a deal?"

"Deal." She threw his arms around her neck.

He pulled away, his black eyes serious but full of love. "And if something happens to me, Claire, always know that I tried my damnedest to come back to you. You have my heart, my love."

She had to swallow hard. "You have my heart, too, my love."

"Good." He had a catch in his voice, as well. "Very, very good."

Epilogue

CLAIRE FELT THE ENGINES downshift even before the captain made her announcement that they were landing at Ronald Reagan International Airport in Washington, D.C. The sight of the huge metropolitan area was quite a shock after a year of seeing nothing but dense green vegetation and occasional brown soil or muddy water from the air.

The sparkling white marble dome of the Capitol building beckoned her home. Her workaholic dad wouldn't be in his office this afternoon, anyway, since he was meeting her plane.

Luc, though. Luc was another story. According to his last e-mail, his team was conducting a major training exercise in the national forest near Ft. Bragg, so she'd have to wait to see him until he had finished.

Despite their physical separation, they had grown closer over the past year, thanks to e-mails and occasional phone calls. He always ended their communications telling her that she had his heart, his special way of telling her he loved her.

Claire grabbed her bags and disembarked. Her

father and their housekeeper Louella held a banner. *Welcome home, Claire.* She ran to her father, holding him tight. "Oh, Dad." She kissed his smoothly shaved cheek and noticed a little more white in his hair. She hoped she hadn't caused it with her year away.

Louella was next in line for a cushiony embrace, exclaiming how tanned and skinny Claire was, promising to cook her favorite foods to plump her up.

Claire smiled. "I'm so glad to see you both. I can't wait to get home."

"We're glad to see you, too." Her dad wrapped his arm around her shoulder. "Now, before we go, we have a surprise for you."

"Really? A welcome-home gift?"

"You could call it that." Dad spun her in a half circle and Luc stepped out from behind a pillar.

Claire covered her mouth in shock and screamed. He wore his dress green uniform, his brand-new Silver Star gleaming above several rows of decoration.

"Welcome back, *cher.*" He opened his arms wide and she sprinted into them, laughing and crying. She dragged his mouth down to hers, the loving touch of his lips like cool, fresh water after a year of thirsting for him. He threaded his fingers into her hair and drank her in, as well.

She could have remained entwined with him forever, but her father's discreet throat-clearing and Louella's sentimental sniffs reminded her they stood on the airport concourse. "What are you doing here? I thought you were out in the field."

"The exercise got canceled last minute and I came to Virginia."

"You should have called me." She grabbed his chin and kissed him again.

He pulled away from her. "I had some business to take care of before I could come meet you." He looked over her shoulder at her father and Louella. "Your papa and I got off on the wrong foot last year, so I wanted to meet him again—and tell him of my intentions."

"Intentions?"

Then she was the only one standing as he dropped to one knee, still holding tight to her hand. "Claire, your father has given his permission to ask for your hand." He reached into his uniform jacket and pulled out a small black box. "Claire, will you marry me?" He pulled out a sparkling white diamond solitaire set in gold.

She covered her mouth again, this time to press back tears of happiness. Instead of putting it on her hand, he tipped up the band so she could read the engraving inside. "*'Vous et nul autre.'*" She pulled the gold chain out from under her shirt that held the matching ring he'd given her a year earlier. "You and no other, Luc."

"*Oui ou non, béb?*" His eyes twinkled at her. "Will you take this rough Cajun soldier for your husband?"

"*Oui.*" He slipped the ring on her fourth finger and she dragged him to his feet for more kisses. "A million times, *oui.*"

We'll be spotlighting a different series every month throughout 2009 to celebrate our 60th anniversary.

Look for Silhouette® Nocturne™ in October!

Travel through time to experience tales that reach the boundaries of life and death. Bestselling authors Lindsay McKenna, Cindy Dees, P.C. Cast and Merline Lovelace join together in a brand-new, four-book Time Raiders miniseries.

TIME RAIDERS

August—*The Seeker*
by *USA TODAY* bestselling author Lindsay McKenna

September—*The Slayer* by Cindy Dees

October—*The Avenger*
by *New York Times* bestselling author and
coauthor of the House of Night novels P.C. Cast

November—*The Protector*
by *USA TODAY* bestselling author Merline Lovelace

Available wherever books are sold.

nocturne™

New York Times bestselling author
and co-author of the House of Night novels

P.C. CAST

makes her stellar debut
in Silhouette® Nocturne™

THE AVENGER

Available October wherever books are sold.

TIME RAIDERS
miniseries

**Bestselling authors Lindsay McKenna,
Cindy Dees, P.C. Cast and Merline Lovelace
come together to bring to life incredible
tales of passion that reach the boundaries
of life and death, in a brand-new
four-book miniseries.**

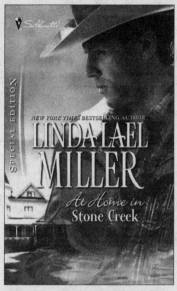

Touch Me

by *New York Times* bestselling author
JACQUIE D'ALESSANDRO

After spending ten years as a nobleman's mistress,
Genevieve Ralston doesn't have any illusions
about love and sex. So when a gorgeous stranger
suddenly decides to wage a sensual assault on her,
who is she to stop him? Little does she guess he'll
want more than her body....

Available October wherever books are sold.

---

red-hot reads

www.eHarlequin.com

HB79499

You're invited to join our Tell Harlequin Reader Panel!

By joining our new reader panel you will:

- Receive Harlequin® books—they are FREE and yours to keep with no obligation to purchase anything!
- Participate in fun online surveys
- Exchange opinions and ideas with women just like you
- Have a say in our new book ideas and help us publish the best in women's fiction

In addition, you will have a chance to win great prizes and receive special gifts!
See Web site for details. Some conditions apply.
Space is limited.

To join, visit us at
www.TellHarlequin.com.

REQUEST YOUR FREE BOOKS!

2 FREE NOVELS PLUS 2 FREE GIFTS!

HARLEQUIN®

Blaze™

Red-hot reads!

YES! Please send me 2 FREE Harlequin® Blaze™ novels and my 2 FREE gifts (gifts are worth about $10). After receiving them, if I don't wish to receive any more books, I can return the shipping statement marked "cancel". If I don't cancel, I will receive 6 brand-new novels every month and be billed just $4.24 per book in the U.S. or $4.71 per book in Canada. That's a savings of 15% off the cover price. It's quite a bargain. Shipping and handling is just 50¢ per book.* I understand that accepting the 2 free books and gifts places me under no obligation to buy anything. I can always return a shipment and cancel at any time. Even if I never buy another book, the two free books and gifts are mine to keep forever.

151 HDN EYS2   351 HDN EYTE

Name	(PLEASE PRINT)	
Address		Apt. #
City	State/Prov.	Zip/Postal Code

Signature (if under 18, a parent or guardian must sign)

Mail to the **Harlequin Reader Service:**
IN U.S.A.: P.O. Box 1867, Buffalo, NY 14240-1867
IN CANADA: P.O. Box 609, Fort Erie, Ontario L2A 5X3

Not valid to current subscribers of Harlequin Blaze books.

**Want to try two free books from another line?
Call 1-800-873-8635 or visit www.morefreebooks.com.**

* Terms and prices subject to change without notice. Prices do not include applicable taxes. N.Y. residents add applicable sales tax. Canadian residents will be charged applicable provincial taxes and GST. Offer not valid in Quebec. This offer is limited to one order per household. All orders subject to approval. Credit or debit balances in a customer's account(s) may be offset by any other outstanding balance owed by or to the customer. Please allow 4 to 6 weeks for delivery. Offer available while quantities last.

Your Privacy: Harlequin Books is committed to protecting your privacy. Our Privacy Policy is available online at www.eHarlequin.com or upon request from the Reader Service. From time to time we make our lists of customers available to reputable third parties who may have a product or service of interest to you. If you would prefer we not share your name and address, please check here. ☐

HB09R3

Stay up-to-date on all your romance reading news!

The Harlequin Inside Romance newsletter is a **FREE** quarterly newsletter highlighting our upcoming series releases and promotions!

Go to eHarlequin.com/InsideRomance or e-mail us at InsideRomance@Harlequin.com to sign up to receive your FREE newsletter today!

COMING NEXT MONTH
Available September 29, 2009

#495 TOUCH ME Jacquie D'Alessandro
Historicals
After spending ten years as a nobleman's mistress, Genevieve Ralston's no stranger to good sex. So when she meets an irresistible stranger with seduction on his mind, she's game. Only little does she guess he wants much more than her body....

#496 CODY Kimberly Raye
Love at First Bite
All Miranda Rivers wants is a simple one-night stand. But when she picks up sexy rodeo star—and vampire—Cody Braddock, that one night might last an eternity....

#497 DANGEROUS CURVES Karen Anders
Undercover Lovers
Distract her rival agent, hot and handsome Max Carpenter, for two weeks—that's Rio Marshall's latest DEA assignment. But in the steamy Hawaiian hideaway, who'll be distracting whom?

#498 CAUGHT IN THE ACT Samantha Hunter
Dressed to Thrill
Wearing a bold 'n' sexy singer's costume has Gina Thomas delivering a standout performance that gives her the chance to search for scandalous photos of her sister. But it also captures the attention of Mason Scott—keeper of said photos. So what will he request when he catches Gina red-handed?

#499 RIPPED! Jennifer LaBrecque
Uniformly Hot!
Lieutenant Colonel Mitch Cooper is a play-by-the-rules kind of guy. Too bad his latest assignment is to keep an eye on free-spirited Eden Walters, who only wants to play...with him!

#500 SEDUCTION BY THE BOOK Stephanie Bond
Encounters
When four Southern wallflowers form a book club, they don't realize they're playing with fire. Because in *this* club, the members are reading classic erotic volumes, learning how to seduce the man of their dreams. After a book or two, Atlanta's male population won't stand a chance!

www.eHarlequin.com

HBCNMBPA0909